Of Necessity and Wanting
Short fictions

Sascha A. Akhtar

Published 2020 by the87press
The 87 Press LTD
87 Stonecot Hill
Sutton
Surrey
SM3 9HJ
www.the87press.com

ISBN: 978-1-8380698-3-4

Design: Stanislava Stoilova [www.sdesign.graphics]

To Karachi,
May the seven saints continue to protect her.

and

Haq Nawaz Akhtar — the original star, who loved her and his beloved Pakistan, above all. You are so missed.

The White Cage

"Outrage in Pakistan after feminism panel includes no women."

— BBC News Story Headline, 22 November 2019.

"Like capitalism, patriarchy is rife with internal contradictions, which leads it to experience periodic crises. Like capitalism, patriarchy will eventually be overthrown."

— Nida Kirmani, 2017.

"The 'disposition to admire, and almost to worship, the rich and the powerful, and to despise, or, at least, to neglect persons of poor and mean condition' is 'the great and most universal cause of the corruption of our moral sentiments."

— Adam Smith, 1759. *The Theory of Moral Sentiments.*

"Submission, subjection or servitude … is very effective in making the man favourably minded towards a woman. It creates pity for her and quenches the fire of his passion. It is applauded by members of both sexes. The greater her submissiveness and her ignorance the greater is the self-importance felt by him. An unfortunate woman devoid of this unique quality is only tolerated if not scorned."

— Iqbalunnisa Hussain, 1944. *Purdah & Polygamy.*

I
Guddi

A Fine Balance

Guddi has a memory that she re-visits often. The sky is a blue canopy emitting a sheen of pure warmth — its hot light penetrating the eyes to the optic core. She is standing on the roof-top of her aunt's sprawling house in the city of Lahore. As far as the eye can travel, there are clusters of people crowded on rooftops silhouetted against the dazzling firmament.

Sound fills the atmosphere almost as much as the sensation of light — shouts, giggles, and yelps of celebration. Guddi looks to the sky and feels her heart whizzing upwards. Bursts of colour emblazon the view — mustard-yellow kites with fluttering cherry-red tails, emerald kites with turquoise tails streaking through the sky, aquamarine, tangerine, amethyst all flying at different heights like a cubist rainbow in the noon-day Lahore sky.

Her father's hair still thick is billowing in the wind, his impressive moustache firmly attached to his face. This is one of the rare occasions that he wears a starched white *shalwar kameez* instead of a bush shirt with trousers.

'Abba! Let me have a go! Let me have a go!' Guddi insists. Abba is thrilled to have his daughter as a companion.

'Now not too tight or the string might break and not too loose or the kite won't fly. It's a balance Guddi,' he tells her.

It takes Guddi a while to get the hang of it. She just cannot make the flappy, papery thing fly and is getting dispirited. But her father patiently stays by her side, holding her hand while flying the kite himself, allowing her to believe it is her doing it. Until Presto!

He deftly removes his hand and it is just she, Guddi flying the kite alone, elated and proud. Her father stands shielding his eyes against the sun with his hand looking into the distance at the kite, tracking its progress.

'I did it, Abba!' Guddi squeals, 'I did it!' Abba is very proud.

'See — it's just a balance. A fine balance,' he says gently — a fine balance between flying and floundering.

Then her irritating cousins Saif and Ari cut her kite down hacking into the string with the ground glass in theirs. Her kite falls with an unceremonious smack on the concrete rooftop, listless and unmoving. Guddi bursts into fat, rolling tears. How the idiots hoot and holler. Abba goes over to them and gives them a piece of his mind.

They are then banned from the rooftop by her bustling aunt.

* * * * * *

'Guddi! Guddi! Are you listening?' Guddi looks up at her mother's face with its layer of assiduously applied make-up — lip-liner, black kohl around the eyes, deep burgundy mehendi-coloured hair wound up on her head and her diamond nose pin winking in the light of the T.V.

'Guddi you really need to take more care of your appearance you know,' her mother continues. She has been talking, Guddi thinks, for what seems like hours about the same things.

'I will take you for a manicure tomorrow. Ok?'

To which Guddi replies dully, 'Yes Amma.' There is

no use arguing. Guddi knows all too well, that to her mother appearance is the be-all and end-all of life.

'And darling — I think we should also get you a facial tomorrow. You're looking a little dark. Have you been in the sun without sunblock?' asks her mother, the evident horror growing on her face at such a vile prospect.

The notion that her daughter might not value keeping her skin as much on the 'fair,' side of 'wheatish,' as possible is unfathomable to Rana Shaukat Khan. Guddi has barely managed to dissuade her mother from forcing her to carry a parasol in the sun like the Victorians, by making her believe that if she did, wouldn't all the Aunties start thinking that she — Guddi, Rana Khan's daughter was — insert sheer terror — not 'fair' enough, and so had to carry a parasol !

This was language her mother understood, and she had never mentioned the parasol again.

So tomorrow after college, she would go and consent to multiple treatments that she couldn't really care less about. But what of it? There wasn't much else to do in this hell-hole of a city anyway — Karachi, the not-so beautiful.

Goray Rang Ka Zamaana:
The Age Of White Skin

The beauty parlour is packed as always with women across the age spectrum. The astringent odours of nail polish and remover mingle with sweet honey wax, pervading the air. The salon owner Shakila sits at the reception desk, her husky, smoky voice resonating through the salon as she converses with a client who has wheeled her parlour chair over to the desk — towel firmly ensconced on her head and two young girls feverishly working to bring the nails of each hand up to par.

The conversations Guddi overheard here were invariably the same — who saw whom where and with whom, marriages gone sour — upcoming nuptials mixed in with some stories of good girls gone 'bad'. You could tell how salacious the gossip was by the timbre of the voices.

Shakila was fed all the gossip that came through — it was an ecosystem. Her cronies who came to the salon would bring whatever delicious tidbits they had as an offering to her, to keep her favour. When her deep voice took on a low rumble, it was clear the subject was particularly scintillating.

With no secrecy or privacy to speak of, the legion of assorted girls who worked in the parlour were privy to everything their clients talked about. Their heads low they looked like they weren't listening but they heard all, important links in the gossip food chain.

The girls then regaled other bored clients with these snippets; they bonded, thus ensuring a good tip. Of course, they also shared with each other and as with any society, sects and tribes developed. The more seasoned girls stuck together and couldn't abide the squeakier, more eager-to-please girls, who delighted in spreading the dirt around wantonly.

There was also client loyalty — rivalries became apparent if one girl's regular customer was given to someone else. The girls prided themselves on building up such a strong rapport with their clients that the women would then return seeking a specific girl by name.

Guddi couldn't stand the fuss that was made over her and the other clients. It seemed Victorian, like the books in school — handmaidens fawning over their wards and the giggling...

These girls could giggle like no-one could — but if there was something that annoyed her above all *it* was how every single time, *a* girl would invariably comment on how 'fair' her mother was and then look over at her, insinuating with gloomy eyes, what a shame it was, that the daughter was not as fair.

Guddi would bite her lip and nod unconvincingly cringing inside. Her mother would say 'Oh it doesn't matter at least she's not black,' and the girls would all giggle — some of whom actually were rather dark-skinned.

'When is Guddi getting married?' Julie would ask slyly and Salma who was massaging Rana Shaukat Khan's feet, on cue, would giggle.

'*Buss jaani.* We'll have to see, darling,' Mrs Shaukat Khan would reply with the sigh of a woman upon whom all the world's woes sat.

'Let her at least finish college. These days boy's families even ask this — if the girl is well-educated or not,' she pronounced the word 'ejyooo-kated,' which Guddi always teased her about.

'Yes, yes Mother ejyoookated, ejyookated, just so I can get married off... Heaven forbid that I should actually do *something* with this education... make something of myself!'

What was this world her mother and most of the housewives of Karachi inhabited? Guddi wondered. It troubled her constantly but some days the absurdity amused.

* * * * * *

As they drive home from the beauty salon, Guddi watches the streets of Karachi — a perpetual frenzy of diverse traffic streaks by. At a red light, myriad flower-sellers— almost exclusively children, descend on their car with delicate, purest white motia flowers, prized for their powerful fragrance, painstakingly strung into chains and bracelets. The *bari gaari-wallahs* liked to hang them from the rearview mirrors. The men often presenting them to the women.

'Baraam, please roll the windows up,' her mother immediately snaps at the driver.

Rolling up the window to the persistent onslaught of all manner of intrusions— black flies, beggars, flower-sellers, vendors of tat — was de *rigeur*. They mobbed the cars vying for attention through the window — as if their life depended on it, because it did. Very often, they would risk chucking their wares into the cars through the open windows, hoping that guilt would make you hastily find that 5 or 10 ruppee note before the light turned green. Many a time, it happened that cars were forced to drive off with goods unpaid for — a risk the flower-sellers needed to take. Good people would sometimes drive back hours later to find the seller & give them the money. It did happen. They were children, after all.

'No, Baraam could you actually purchase a string of flowers for me, please?' Guddi asks. Whenever they are out with Abba, he gets her a bracelet of these, her favourite flowers, the car instantly filling up with their potent perfume.

The driver dutifully buys a few strands, handing them back to her. She cups them in her hands, inhaling deeply.

'You are still such a child,' her mother says gently.

* * * * * *

'So, where have you ladies been this evening?' Guddi's father asks them over dinner.

Guddi rolls her eyes 'Abba where do you think?'

'Shopping? No? Aah I see,' her father says knowingly 'Bee-yoo-ti-fication! I don't know why you bother. You already are the most bee-yoo-ti-fool girl in the world!'

'Shaukat stop putting ideas in her head!' Rana Shaukat Khan, snaps.

'I am not putting ideas in her head!' he winks at Guddi.

'Am I not allowed to believe that my only daughter is Theee Most Bee-yoo-ti-fool? Why do you insist on getting such a young girl beautified and what-not all the time anyway? *Haina* Ami Jaan? Right Mother Darling?'

He turns to his octogenarian mother who is wearing a modest white, cotton *kameez-shalwar* — a *dupatta* covering her hair, the colour of the *motia* flower. Ami Jaan is busily making *niwalas* of rice and meat with her fingers — deftly feeding these hand-made balls of food into her mouth in two swift motions. She looks up from her work to give him a pointed glare.

'Shaukat please don't discuss such topics at mealtimes.

Guddi is well aware that I have no interest in such conversation.'

Guddi's mother shoots a smug look at her husband and they proceed to eat in silence — the only sound the cricket match blaring on the television.

3

California Dreamin'

There *were* other lives out there — she knew it. Other countries, other cities — cooler, cleaner places. Cities with palm trees lining the avenues that actually *lived and* thrived, unlike the dehydrated, sad ghosts of trees that lined the Karachi streets — caught in an endless cycle of replanting & death. The city hired gardeners to plant them, but without constant water, nothing could survive.

She knew there *were* places where things looked fresh, vibrant — alive. Places where the canals were not clogged with raw sewage, rendering them a nasty shade of green as they were in her city — canals with sparkling waters and houseboats on them, in which people actually dwelt. Places with air. Actual air that could be breathed. The smell of Karachi, was an odour most pungent. There was no escape from it. The roundabout to Clifton Bridge reeked of fish rotting 24 hours a day. The trucks that crossed by transported high volumes of them from the ports. Within the internal lanes of Clifton, the fish aroma was overpowered by raw sewage, and come evening by smog, from all the rattling exhaust pipes on the mammoth ailing trucks — resplendent and artful on the outside but in truth — death-traps.

The atmosphere in the evening, would become a veritable symphony of stench, so much so that Guddi would often not want to leave the cool vacuum of her father's air-conditioned Honda Civic when they parked anywhere. Baraam Driver could go into the shops and get whatever she needed — a DVD from the pirated DVD store, a *paan*, deftly wrapped in betel leaves — whatever — she would wait in the car.

Even Lahore wasn't this bad. Islamabad, she thought, was like paradise by comparison but the place she dreamt of the most was called Melrose Place. She watched season after season of the American show on DVD and had done so for years. How shiny everything looked, even the people.

The girls postured like they'd been painted by a painter with an impeccable eye for symmetry and proportion, who then breathed life into them. Guddi would sit at her dressing table for hours staring into her mirror.

No, her teeth were definitely not as white as theirs. How was it possible for people to have such white teeth? All the girls were the colour of smooth and silky milk — with hair that cascaded down their backs like liquid sunlight.

As she examined her own face in the mirror, she wondered what she would look like if she was the colour of milk. She scrutinized her reflection in the mirror.

Surely, she was reasonably attractive? But those girls, those girls on Melrose Place seemed to Guddi to look so clean and crystalline: *like angels*, she thought.

Guddi was convinced that in Melrose Place the air would smell of coconuts and frangipani. It was all that clean air they breathed that made them so pale and beautiful — she was sure of it.

Sometimes she imagined it as the mirror-world of Karachi; similar but opposite. Karachi was California gone rotten. Here the buildings never looked new for longer than a few months. It was as if the air of Karachi was intent on disintegration. Dust got in everywhere, paint started peeling and the rust... there was no escaping rust in Karachi.

The sea made that impossible. There was no rust though, in Melrose Place, or fish, or dirt, or mothers who were obsessed with their daughters being fair; because there, everyone was fair.

At night whilst falling asleep, she would imagine this alternate-universe Karachi and like Alice, fall down the rabbit hole. Dreaming of the white princesses of Melrose Place, who would offer her frosted pink cupcakes — the kind you only ever saw in Western magazines — that would change her into one of them and keep her there forever.

* 4 *

Bad Things

There was a buzz going around her all-girls' college that Somaiya, the girl who was considered 'loose' because she was rumoured to hang out with 'boys', was having a party at her house.

'I wonder what it'll be like?' Kiran waggled her eyebrows at Guddi.

'Well, I'm sure it would be fun,' Maliha said yearningly. Her parents like most of the girl's parents in their social circle, never let her go to parties or anywhere unaccompanied for that matter.

'Yah,' said Tabassum, 'probably wouldn't be booooring'.

'Definitely NOT boring!' Rabia added.

'But where will Somaiya's parents be? Don't they disapprove of this kind of thing?' Guddi asked worriedly.

'Somaiya's parents are never there, *yaar*!' replied Rabia, 'her dad is some rich businessman who is always in Singapore and her mother is always out at dinner parties and *falana dhumkana*. They don't know what their daughter is up to!'

'Well I have something to tell you guys!' Kiran suddenly piped up.

'WHAT?' the voices rang in unison. 'Somaiya's younger sister is friends with my cousin and if we want to go to the party... we can!' The girl's mouths dropped. They did not get invited to parties, resigned as they were, to being from nerdy, conservative families. Kiran's parents alone came without a restricted mind-set based in pseudo-religious dogma.

'Let's go!'

'Don't be mad Kiran!' Guddi was alarmed by her friends' urgency. Sure they talked about parties but no-one ever actually wanted to go to one... did they?

'Anyway, there's no way I would be able to go,' she added primly.

'Yeah me neither,' Tabassum said gloomily, 'I'd never get permission.'

'Hmmm...' said Rabia.

'You know,' Kiran said slyly: 'I heard that Somaiya's elder brother is really ceeyooote and he's going to be there!'

'Can we convince our brothers to take us? Our parents don't mind too much if they're there?' Rabia turned to Kiran.

'Shut up *yaar*,' Maliha said agitated but excited.

'Ooh!' Kiran's interest was piqued.

'You guys are proper *paagal*!' There was a general round of schoolyard-style excitement in the form of ribbing & teasing, before the bell rang for them to get back into class.

Guddi strode ahead purposefully, eager to end what she viewed as a lost cause of a conversation. She wasn't sure she wanted to go anyway — who knew what occurred at these parties. And although curious, she felt a rather generalized anxiety around the whole thing. She knew some of her friends climbed down drain-pipes along the sides of their homes or had replicas of their house keys made without their parents' knowledge, in order to engage in stealthy operations to leave their homes, for rendezvous with obviously sketchy characters of the male persuasion. Well, to her mind, all men seemed sketchy.

Aunty 'Gurriya' (which was the less vernacular and proper form of 'Guddi', or 'doll', also used a nick-name) a raucous divorcee whom her mother knew from Shak's beauty salon had once said: 'There are two things you can never trust *beti* — Pakistani water & Pakistani men' — waggling a perfectly manicured fuchsia nail in her face, and it had stuck.

Sneaking out of her house was out of the question. Guddi did not have the requisite nerve to incur the wrath of Rana Khan and neither did she have the strength of purpose. The girls on Melrose Place were bad. They did bad things. But Guddi reluctantly admitted to herself that she was perhaps just a 'good' girl — good and perhaps she suspected, even a little boring for a girl of 18.

Her best friend Kiran, on the other hand was definitely exciting. Rabia too also seemed to have a life; they socialized outside their circle. They had other friends that they met for *chaat*, for burgers, for drives along the Clifton beachside — for dinner. Both Rabia and Kiran had the advantage of brothers who chaperoned them. Kiran tried constantly to draw Guddi out of her shell and to empower her to stand up to her mother.

'You're a grown woman for God's sake Guddi! What is this bullshit, *na*?' But Guddi knew deep down that she was just fated for a different life from Kiran.

Kiran's parents were proper liberal, educated and they had genuine hopes for their daughter, beyond matrimony.

They were willing to let her travel abroad, to the United States or the United Kingdom to study if she was able to secure a scholarship. Kiran's mother wasn't constantly scheming to marry her off and this Guddi envied above all.

Kiran had options. Options available to her, unlike Guddi, who had none. Kiran talked with confidence of having a job someday. She wasn't sure what it would be yet, and that in itself amazed Guddi.

Guddi's mother had taught her that she should never have to work. That she would be married to a prosperous man and there was no question of a distasteful 'job'. In true fact, the idea of independence intrigued Guddi. She fantasized about just getting up and going and being anything, anything at all besides the property of a man.

As much as the girls in the beauty parlours got under her skin, she was secretly fascinated by them. They got up, left their houses — they could be anywhere for all their parents knew! They earned their own money, and in many cases supported their families.

'I wonder what that feels like?' Guddi mused, often 'I wonder... what... that... feels... like?'

5

Self-Loathing

Most afternoons Ami Jaan could be found sitting smoking her hookah on a takht in her sparsely decorated room. It contained an uncomfortable-looking single bed, dressed in old, fading linen and a prayer rug worn at the spots where the forehead and knees had had countless encounters with the pile of the small, rectangular carpet in prostration.

There was also an antique, wooden sideboard that was the one possession she had brought with her from her village in Sargodha. Atop the sideboard were a discoloured, orange comb, three *tasbis* wrought of three different kinds of material respectively — *firoza*, carnelian and earth, her trusty mustard-seed oil (that she used for treating all manner of ailment, aches & pains), and a faded sepia photograph of Guddi's father. A young man beaming out of the frame, sporting lamb chops on his face. Abba had apparently been a village 'dude'.

'Always dreaming!' Ami Jaan would say of him when prompted to tell stories of his youth. She was clearly proud of how he had left the village to seek his fortune and become a 'bijness' man in the city. 'And now with God's grace see this house, his bijness (business), his big car!'

His father had died when he was merely a teenager and Ami Jaan refused to allow him to give up his dreams and stay on in the village in order to take care of her and his siblings. She had pulled out from under her bed, a cloth bundle full of rupees that she had been putting aside for well over 30 years. This, she gave to him and set him off on his way. He had gone to Lahore to work for a distant relative who owned a fabric shop. Now, he managed a mill for a powerful textile magnate.

'Your father did this all for you child,' Ami Jaan would say to Guddi.

Guddi spent her afternoons after college, with Ami Jaan pressing her legs for hours on end, rubbing in the beloved mustard-seed oil. It did not have the loveliest of fragrances, but to Ami Jaan, it was a comforting and familiar smell. Her grandmother disapproved of her daughter-in-law's values. But being a woman prone to peaceful environments — had made the decision never to intefere.

'You know your Abba is right Rumina,' Ami Jaan said to her one day whilst she lay half-asleep in the afternoon heat, calling her by her given name. 'All this importance on how you look is just ridiculous. The way God has made you is A-Vun!'

Ami Jaan loved saying A-One. She had picked it up from a nephew and relished throwing this English colloquialism into her conversations followed by a throaty cackle that only a woman of her years, who smoked a hookah could have cultivated.

Guddi smiled and nodded.

'*Ji* Ami Jaan. Yes, Ami Dear.'

'What have you done to your hair?'

Ami Jaan rustled her granddaughter's straight, silky hair so it flew up in the air and then fell back on her shoulders.

'What do you mean Ami Jaan?' After all, she *had* fought some not inconsiderable battles with her mother to at the very least ensure, the hairstyle she had did not render her a absolute *identical* clone of the other socialites on the

Karachi scene.

'Well, your hair isn't naturally this straight now, is it Rumina?' She looked at Guddi with eyes wide and eyebrows raised comically.

'No. But... but...' Guddi trailed off.

'But what? If you spend so much time on hair and face, who will tend to your mind? Your mind will fly away with all this blow-drying!' Rumina laughed.

In plain fact, Guddi *did* abhor her curly hair and nearly every girl and woman she knew in Karachi had their hair straightened, plus her mother had always insisted on it. She wanted Guddi to stay trendy so that ultimately, she would be desirable to a man from an elite family, and thus Rana Shaukat Khan could accomplish her mission in life to make Guddi a member of the Karachi Princesses Club (and thus earn a spot in the Karachi Glam Matriarch's Club).

'What does your mother want? For you to become like all these other useless women?' Ami Jaan said as if reading her thoughts.

'That you should frequent fancy hotels and live in a big house in Defence?'

When Ami Jaan decided to address the things that Guddi spoke to no-one else about, Guddi would look at Ami Jaan's lined face relieved to have this woman in her life. She was like a lighthouse in the conflicting storm of her emotions, cutting through the haze that sometimes came over her eyes as she sacrificed herself up more and more to her pre-ordained life.

She loved it that Ami Jaan called her Rumina. She wished her parents would stop calling her Guddi — 'Doll'.

'Rumina you can be anyone you want,' Ami Jaan said gently, 'You don't have to fit a mould. Your destiny will come to you. You can't force it. None of these things your mother cares so much for are important.'

All that is important is that you are happy. A man can be rich or poor, he can be a simple man or a grand man but if he is not a good man, a kind man, a gentle man... Well... there's just no use having a bad husband for the sake of wealth.'

* 6 *

Dil Ka Rang:
The Colour Of The Heart

It was when Guddi was 16, that Amma started dragging her round to a joyless string of luncheons, tea parties, gatherings and shopping trips that she would grow increasingly weary of. The other *begums* would bring their daughters along too, and they would experience collective ennui, whilst their mothers cooed, talking amongst themselves about them as if they weren't right there. What they talked about was men — marriable men — sons, brothers, grandsons — these events, of which you could be sure many more were being held around the country, very possibly simultaneously — were like horse and cattle shows. Tips and leads were shared. Alliances and partnerships were forged. Enemies were identified.

Guddi could pinpoint the events that led to her mother's change. She had been overjoyed when Abba's boss offered them a company house in Clifton with a car and driver. They were not given possession of these but they got out of Gulshan-I-Iqbal and that was all that Rana Khan could hope and dream of.

Steadily, her mother became a P.R agent, getting herself invited places, burrowing her way 'in' further and further. 'Guddi *jaan* we have to go to Asma Chidoy's luncheon for ladies, or we have to go to Kerroo Saijol's exhibition of clothing at the Marriot'. She stopped meeting all her friends from the old neighbourhood — like Aunty Kausar, a kind, gentle dough-shaped lady with three equally mild and bready daughters.

Aunty Kausar was not in the least bit glamorous. She wore her hair parted in the middle and tied back in a wiry ponytail. Far from the latest fashions, she wore shapeless mix silk and polyester *shalwar kameezzes*; a chiffon *dupatta* always on her head.

Abba asked periodically, 'I haven't seen Kausar in a while,' or 'Why don't you invite Kausar over?' completely oblivious to the fact that his wife was consciously eliminating all the Aunty Kausars from her life to make way for the Grande Dames of the Karachi social scene. Guddi wondered if he was aware but just didn't want to get involved. When Abba asked such questions, Ami Jaan would raise her eyebrows and look at Guddi pointedly. Guddi would look away shamedly.

Rana Khan would say something like, 'Yes, Kausar has been quite busy as of late.' Ami Jaan rarely commented, despite being fully aware of everything that went on in her daughter-in-law and granddaughters' lives.

Amma was in a particularly chirpy mood at dinner. Guddi knew this was because she had heard at the ladies gala luncheon through Aunty Nusrat that Aunty Jamila had said that Durriya Dadabhoy had commented on how pretty Guddi was, having seen her at Aunty Minty's tea party.

Durriya Dadabhoy was a rich and powerful woman, but most importantly she had not one, not two, but three sons! For Rana, this one seemingly stray comment felt like an investment paying back, all the countless facial treatments to ensure Guddi's skin was top-notch and a desirable shade. All the time and energy expended in procuring invitations to social gatherings were finally reaping returns.

Durriya Dadabhoy was famous for keeping an eye out for girls for her sons and she was also very, very finicky and never commented about just anybody, after all. Her mother had relayed all this to her in the car on the way home from the gala, whilst Guddi stared out of the window. Her mother clearly seemed excited. But it had scarcely dawned on Guddi that her mother was actually talking about her, Guddi/Rumina and her future prospects to a real flesh and blood guy. She had cultivated a careful disconnection from her own life and at times it was difficult to return to her body.

'I met your old friend Mrs. Qazim today,' Abba said at dinner.

'Acha? Oh?' said her mother distractedly at the mention of one of her Gulshan-i-Iqbal cronies.

'Yes, she was asking about you and wondered why you hadn't called in so long,' he added.

'Your wife has new friends now,' Ami Jaan chimed in uncharacteristically.

'Well so it would seem,' Abba replied light-heartedly, 'But Mrs. Qazim was very interested in what a certain Miss Guddi was up to,' he winked at his daughter, 'as she is looking for a suitable girl for her Mohsin.'

Rana Khan nearly choked on the piece of chicken she had been chewing.

'Mohsin!' she exploded, 'Guddi *jaani* do you remember him?' Guddi had only a vague memory of Mrs. Qazim's son, and shook her head.

'He is even darker-skinned than yourrr father!' she said in alarm rolling her r's. This was the gauge by which Rana determined how 'dark', someone's skin was, for she had decided that her very own husband was the absolute measure of 'darkness'. Guddi always found this hilarious, as did her father.

'Yes, yes Guddi. Don't you know your father is an absolute black devil!' He mocked himself, laughing with abandon at the look of sheer terror on his wife's face.

Only Ami Jaan was not amused, 'So what? Do you know the complexion of a man's heart by the colour of his skin?' Rana had an uneasy truce with her mother-in-law and this comment confused her.

'Mother, who is talking about a man's heart? I just want that our Guddi finds a rich boy with a big house...' Ami Jaan interrupted her, 'Rana you neither know your daughter, nor do you wish her happiness. You just want to make her into a copy of yourself.'

The words sliced through the atmosphere in the dining room. Nobody spoke. Guddi looked into her plate nervously not daring to look at her mother. Ami Jaan however, seemed to be in a dangerous mood.

'Shaukat, why don't you talk to your wife? She parades the girl around like a show-horse. She is trying to rub out her personality! Guddi is just a child. Let her study! Let her decide what she wants from her life! She is your only daughter for Allah's sake!'

Shaukat Khan found himself in an uncomfortable position. He was being forced to engage with the workings of his family, something he was not often called upon to do. 'Amma,' he said softly 'whatever makes Guddi happy.'

'Forget it!' Ami Jaan got up slowly, purposely from the table, 'The two of you have nothing to teach Rumina.'

For a moment Guddi had wanted her father to say something to her mother; to stand up to her. But he just said what he always did, and the moment passed. In a way Guddi was relieved. The pressure of radically altering the status quo would have been too much. But what had Ami Jaan meant about a man's heart?

7

Ladies' Timing

There was also that movie, *Bend It Like Beckham,* that she had seen at a friend's house. The film had a desi girl in it, Indian or Pakistani, who had wanted to be a football player and had succeeded! Guddi sat on the wooden Sindhi *jhoola* on her terrace swaying back and forth cradling her knees as the sun set. The pleasantly creaking sound of the large wooden swing mingled with early crickets. A woman football player. She had never even heard of one in Pakistan. She certainly didn't know one. Or a cricket player or a squash player or any sports 'woman', for that matter.

Girls did have sports in school, but sporting as a life choice was just not an option. She wondered if it was a religious thing, but hadn't there been a story on the news the other day about an Irani women's judo team that competed on a national level, won medals. They were certainly the most 'Islamic' country she knew of. The images in the news report had seemed so bizarre, the women's heads all covered in hijab and the rest of them in Martial Arts clothes. Bizarre, yet strangely exciting. Nothing had stopped, what was her name, Toktam Bidel from becoming a martial arts champion, and hadn't the report said her husband was supportive of her?

The Islam of Iran seemed a far cry from the Islam of Pakistan in Guddi's mind. Certainly, she didn't want to be forced to wear hijab but wouldn't it be cool to see women participating in male dominated sports?

She swung back and forth watching the bougainvillea in their garden change tones in the waning sun, wondering if there was bougainvillea in Melrose Place. A classmate had family in America and regaled them with stories of her summer vacations. She talked of clean beaches and women who wore whatever they wanted and *no staring*.

'My mother and I actually swam in the sea!'

At the beaches of Karachi, the likelihood of seeing women swim in bathing suits was nil to zero. Women usually splashed about standing in the water fully clothed; swimming was *door ki baat* — a possibility so far-fetched it was as good as none.

At the slightly more 'exclusive' beaches every so often girls from more liberal families might wear shorts and a t-shirt but for a woman to truly feel liberated, enjoy the water, absorb sunshine into her skin whilst laying on the sand was next to impossible. Unless it was in a segregated pool at one of the exclusive clubs.

For the most part it was considered 'un-islamic' or simply wasn't permitted by the husbands, brothers, fathers uncles — the patriarchal ruling element of society.

Some of the women who would not have a problem wearing swim gear and swimming were too self-conscious to do so — burnt from years of being heckled and eye-fucked by men in the bazaars, in the streets, having their bums pinched or worse still swoops of alien hands swiping between the legs, unseen.

Ick, Guddi thought. She detested going to Saddar, or any of the bustling markets for this very reason. Why does it bother you so much *yaar*? Kiran would ask. Just ignore them! Or better yet abuse them! Kiran had picked up some gems of swear-words from her very strong-minded, no-nonsense mother. One was: *Apni Mah -behen ko ja ke dhek*. Which

26

translated roughly to: *Why don't you go eye-fuck your mother or sister?*

You see, that was the only thing that could snap them out of it — recall some shred of their decency. It worked a treat. But it also caused them to puff up and grow indignant on occasion. Bringing up a man's female relationships was one of the worst insults a woman could hurl at him — calling upon shame and guilt to force the man in question to behave. When they didn't like it, they didn't like it. Not one bit.

'How dare you!' they would say, turning proper evil (didn't take much to see the ugly face hidden below a thin veneer), 'A woman who is not my mother or sister — talk of my mother and sister...' (never mind that I am openly leching on you).

Once the mother or sister card was played all bets were off. But even Kiran didn't have the nerve to use the B or M word; *behnchod sisterfucker* or *maachod* motherfucker which were the best insults if in a particularly irksome bind and were heard on the lips of men all over Pakistan as commonly as 'shit'. When a woman uttered them though, it was particularly potent.

Guddi could not explain fully to Kiran, why she could not ignore the unwelcome male attention that was part of life in Pakistan. Her mother too was more resilient than her in this regard. But Guddi loathed it.

She thought of the beaches that Anila had told her of in America. Guddi was disgusted by the beaches in Karachi. They were dirty, smelt bad and she had never thought that beaches could actually be fun except on television and in films. In Melrose Place, the teenagers seemed to live on immaculate beaches with delicious-looking water; a far cry from the grey-black oil-slicked, rubbish-laden sands that crowned the seashore.

Would she wear a sparkly bright swimsuit and swim in the sea? She might, thought Guddi. She knew how to swim, thanks to Abba who insisted when she was little that she learn.

Every week his friend Uncle Ikram took his own family to the exclusive Gymkhana Club, and invited them. When she got older and felt uncomfortable swimming in front of men, even her father, she started going with friends who were members of Gymkhana for the Ladies' Timing swim sessions. She never felt more alive then when she was able to remove her clothes, get into the clean blue pool and swim away. It was when she felt most free. Her mother, on the other hand, would not be caught dead in a bathing suit.

The *jhoola's* melodic wooden groans continued as it swung back and forth. The night-lights in the garden and around the house came on automatically. Guddi continued to imagine swimming in a crystalline California ocean, running out onto clean biscuit-coloured sands and collapsing to lay down in a toasty sun for a nap.

She could smell the ocean, and hear the waves lapping as she fell asleep swinging back and forth on her garden terrace in Karachi.

8

The Invention Of Artifice

Guddi knew that despite her mother's best efforts she could not magically erase the fact that they were not in fact rich or powerful people like the families she tried to get in with. She hadn't gone to the prestigious Karachi Grammar School. They only owned one car, and even that was a company car. They had never been abroad for a holiday and her parents spoke atrocious English.

But then her mother started lying. Guddi didn't notice at first but slowly grew more aware of it. A comment here from Aunty Faiza, 'So darling I hope you and your mother enjoy your shopping trip to London!'

A comment there from Aunty Nayyar's very spoilt and incredibly beautiful daughters, 'So your mom has started buying your dowry all from Sono & Shahnaz? Wow!'

Guddi would find herself dumbfounded by these comments and initially thought there was some misunderstanding and would just smile mutely. Even through more and more of these incidents accumulating, followed by her actually catching her mother in the act — she continued to smile.

She was surrounded constantly by the smooth-skinned bejewelled women at the luncheons, smelling exquisitely fresh from trips to the salon, travelling to New York for their son Booji's graduation or to London just to chill out, or to Dubai to shop for Ni-Ni's wedding — and then it happened; Guddi began to lie too.

It started out small at first about restaurants that she had eaten at — Oh yes she had eaten at **Sakura,** the posh

Japanese restaurant, and she frequented Café Flo. But as she started becoming heady with the power of the lies and identifying with her fabrications, Her lies grew in volume (and mass). It was as if she had discovered a map to a forbidden island.

Things got sticky when she lied about being a member of Sindh Club, the most exclusive 'Members Only' leisure club — a colonial-era outlier in the social landscape. 'Really? But I am there every day for ladies swimming I don't think I've seen you there!'

'Oh yes,' Guddi covered up, 'Actually I haven't been in a loong time, because I've been trying out SHAPES you know?' SHAPES was the new gym in town, that she had heard people talking about. The truth was she had never actually set foot in a gym.

'Oh — I see!'

'*Haan* yes It's just sooo much nicer than Sindh Club you know?' Guddi added with an imperious flourish.

'You should try it out.' In accordance with Guddi and her mother's web of lies, they were a loaded extremely privileged family related to Rajput royalty who once lived in Bahrain where her husband was working, 'in oil you know,' until they re-located to Pakistan, 'to be near family,' sometime in the early 90's.

It was easy to live a made-up life. The people she was lying to lived in a bubble and unless there was something obvious to gossip about, took no interest in the details. It was a self-obsessed world with invites to prestigious unions being the Holy Grail.

Of course, the irony was that people often showed up uninvited to weddings. It was the done thing. Planning for a set number of people was unheard of. If one thought there might be 200 people chances are there would be 500. The trick was to make sure the space was massive and keep the food a-comin'. Weddings were where it seemed people ate for the rest of the year.

The custom dictated that guests had to wait two maybe three hours to eat, which was the time needed for the bride to make her mandatory late appearance onto the stage. When they arrived, bride and groom would proceed to sit on a stage, on a throne, adorned with flower arrangements, lights, brocades and backdrops.

They would stay in that position, in heavily bejewelled clothing — the groom's head often adorned with an absurdly tall hat constructed of swathes of fabric — *pagris* — or worse, a curtain of flowers *hiding his* face, for the entirety of the evening. Family, friends, well-wishers would come up to congratulate the couple, attempt to make small-talk whilst on display. Hot flashes of light would go off constantly; photographers took pictures and the videographers danced. No high-status wedding left undocumented.

The tableau-vivant unfolding — off-stage the guests growing restless: *When do we eat? When do we eat?*

The wait was part of the game. Once the food was served the buffet tables would be stormed. The large, imposing matriarchs women who would stride over in tight silks, gold bangles clanking — to the buffet tables as soon as food was laid out— were the most intimidating. Nobody got past them: The Aunties (who would be returning for second helpings of oil-soaked biryani and kebabs).

This same protocol was repeated for the *Valima*, on the third day, of the multi-day wedding extravaganza. The only difference was that the bride and groom would invariably appear more relaxed having surmounted the hurdle of the much-touted 'wedding night', but saddled with the ignominy of *knowing* that everyone else *knew and relished* the fact that *a marriage had been consummated* (in some fashion). This was an opportunity for all the women to comment and observe how the bride was looking *now that she and the groom had bonked* — basically.

There was always a rogue faction at the weddings — those who would slip off and down gallons of smuggled scotch, vodka, rum in their cars, or ensconced in one of the myriad rooms in the mansion — or in bushes, which did in a pinch. You could tell who the party people were. They were the ones who appeared to be having the best time and inevitably comprised of those closest to the wedding parties — the male friends, cousins and siblings of the groom and the female friends, cousins and siblings of the bride celebrating the union in *true* Pakistani fashion. Never underestimate a Pakistani's ability to party.

And that would be pretty much that, except for the next day of course, and for a few weeks after that — there would be the talk. 'Did you see how Aliya Khan's daughter was behaving at Rukaiya and Salman's wedding? Oh my god!' Or: 'Oh yes I was at Jeena Munir's wedding. Oh my god how lovely she looked so elegant. *Haan Haan,* Sono & Shahnaz bridal wear, *darrling.* What a shame you couldn't be there!' Or: 'What was (X,Y, Z) wearing!' Or: 'Did you see what (X, Y, Z) was wearing!' But the most important social function that weddings fulfilled was giving the grande-dames of Karachi the opportunity to check out prospective matches for their sons and daughters.

There were, of course, only so many weddings one could attend in a week. You didn't want to be seen too often and become old hat, and you didn't want to not be seen and be forgotten. The biggest problem of all if you were a woman was, of course, attire. Rana Khan could simply not afford to purchase an endless supply of designer clothes in which to parade her daughter, so she rotated the clothes *strategically*.

She knew which circles frequented which weddings and so knew when it *would* be okay to wear the same clothing again *and* avoid embarrassment. However, with this fine line they were treading between truth and reality, at times the margin for error was too great.

'Amma! Amma!' Guddi was shrieking through the house for her mother.

'What happened *beti* why are you yelling like a madwoman?'

'Amma I am in Eye Spy!'

Every society must have their society pages and Weekend Talk was just such a rag that printed rows and rows of photographs of Tom, Dick, Harry — Tinkoo, Pinkoo, Bubloo laughing it up at social events (that everyone and no-one *really* cared about. Well almost no-one, for there were the *begums* for whom it was rapidly becoming the Rosetta Stone of socializing.

People invited the photographers of the 'Eye Spy' pages into their private parties just to have their photos appear in the magazine. Others sent in blurry photos taken surreptitiously with their mobile phones. Depending on the prestige factor, even the blurriest of photos would be printed.

The photographs were accompanied, by the names of the people. Sometimes it said: X, Y, Z with 'Guest'. That usually irked 'Guest'; indicating that they were not important enough to find out their names and not well-known enough that their name would be known.

The magazine was neither glitzy nor glam, printed on paper closely related to newspaper — the quality of the images was most often poor, as when a photograph was hurriedly pulled off someone's phone and had had the pixels jacked up — but to those who liked to see and be seen; it was theirs and they loved it.

Now Guddi had officially 'arrived'. A few months previously she had appeared in Eye Spy. But much to Rana's chagrin it was as 'Guest'. At the time they'd taken what they could get. To hear she was in it again was a definite cause for celebration.

'Amma — I am in the same outfit I wore to Tooba's wedding!' Guddi said sombrely.

'Well it was a few weeks ago *jaani*, doesn't matter. After all, it is your best outfit.'

To her mother the good news was that Guddi had really made it this time. In small black print under her photo it read 'Guddi.'

The Guddi in question was, however, none too pleased with this. It was too generic and assumed that everyone would know who the 'Guddi' in question was. It made her sound like some kind of hanger-on or good-time-girl, she thought — the kind who only has one ridiculous pet name like Coochi, or Toochi or Munnu.

'That's it Amma!' she said petulantly.

'Please just stop calling me Guddi now. My name is Rumina!' And so Rumina finally assumed her own identity. Her father still called her Guddi though and that was alright.

Rumina's friends didn't come over as much anymore.

'I hardly ever see you *yaar*!' Kiran would bemoan. She

and Rabia were the two out of their group who had attended Somaiya's Party — accompanied by their brothers. That event had set off a whole spiral of events that were shaping Kiran's path into one that was wholly in contrast Rumina's.

As for Maliha and Tabassum, well, like Rumina, they were being groomed by their mothers. Once in a while she did run into them at weddings and it was always a lot more fun for their presence. But for the most part their grooming involved a great deal less social climbing than hers. The friends still socialized in college occasionally. Rumina realized a little ashamedly, that they didn't interest her anymore because they didn't know the names of the people she wanted to talk about — they didn't particularly care about the important designers, and she couldn't gossip with them anymore.

'Wow Rumina your hair has become *really* light!' Rabia commented one day. Rumina had steadily gone from one streak of light in her dark hair to adding more and more till her hair was that shade of golden-blonde that dark-haired people who wanted to lighten their hair had to be satisfied with. She had fully appropriated the uniform of the Karachi socialite. Her mother told her it made her skin, which she continued to subject to regular bleaching treatments, *appear even* lighter.

'Yeah and your eyebrows are always purrrrfect!' Tabassum chimed in, commenting on the permanently alarmed arch of Rumina's eyebrows.

'Well don't you know our old friend Rumina has become a clone!' interjected Kiran to which Rumina looked at her pointedly,

'What exactly do you mean?'

'Rumina you're not you anymore!'

'I am very much me thank you Kiran. At least I'm not going to parties wearing god-knows-what and drinking!'

Rumina's words were uttered more viciously than even she had anticipated — her carefully constructed personality had felt threatened by Kiran's comments. Kiran laughed.

'Oh yeah "God-knows – What." Why? Just because I'm not wearing the much-coveted 'Riaz Babar' and 'Sono and Shahnaz' clothes and just because I'm not trying to become a Pakistani Barbie doll! I never expected this from you Guddi!'

'Don't call me Guddi!'

'Why not? You are a 'Guddi'!'

'Look Kiran just come off it okay.' 'No — you come off it!'

Rabia and Tabassum looked from one to the other, not daring to interfere.

'There's nothing wrong with wanting a different life Kiran,' Rumina said in a rare moment of honesty.

'There is something wrong when that different life involves becoming a different person,' Kiran retorted.

'I'm NOT a DIFFERENT person!' Rumina yelled.

'To hell with you!' She walked off. She didn't need this from these nobody's. 'What did they know anyway?' Something inside her though was murmuring, a little troubled, the way she felt when Ami Jaan talked to her.

* * * * * *

'Happy Birthday... Happy Bird-day to you... Happy Bird-day Dear Gudd... Ruminaa!... Happy Birth-a--day to you!' The three voices of her mother, father and grandmother sang to her in different cadences, calling her by different names. It was her 19th birthday and they had got her a cake. They were going out for dinner to China Town. Rumina inwardly rolled her eyes.

Not China Town, she thought — it was so... pedestrian.

'Abba,' she said working all her only-daughter charm on her unwitting father. 'Pleeease can we go somewhere else for my birthday?' Her father took one look at her and acquiesced.

'Of course, Guddi anywhere you want!' Rumina shot her mother a look. 'Can we go to **Sakura**?'

Her father looked surprised, **Sakura**? That Japanese place in the Excelsior Crown hotel?

'But Guddi will we even like Japanese food?'

'Of course Shaukat, it's just like Chinese no?' Rana snapped at him.

'Oh no not Japanese food. They eat raw fish, child.' Ami Jaan added worriedly. 'Yes, they do Ami Jaan, but we don't have to eat that. They have lots of different things on their menu you know!' Rumina tried to reassure her.

Her father gave in, mentally making a note to take his credit card with the highest credit limit. He had heard that the bill at this '**Sakura**' could go into the double-digit thousands. He would take her, why not, it wasn't as if there were that many fancy restaurants in Karachi — he couldn't blame his daughter for wanting to see what all the fuss was about.

God knows the poor girl hardly ever went out without her mother.

II
Rumina

* 1 *

The White Cage

In the dream, the moonlight is so bright that it creates the illusion of day. There are hundreds of kites in every shade of blue and yellow set against the night vista. She is jumping up and down on the rooftop of a magnificent palace trying to catch them but they are flying too high. A huge figure is silhouetted against the moonlight, obviously a giant.

He is walking towards her. She feels anxious but not afraid and stands rooted to the spot. As his face becomes visible she recognizes him and smiles. It's Abba! Abba! she cries. Abba's massive hands come down towards her and with one hand he gingerly lifts her up onto the palm of the other. He stands up and lifts his palm towards the moon.

Her heart beats faster. When his hand reaches the kites, he stops so that she can easily reach for them. She clutches one in her hand, which is tiny by comparison. But the minute she touches it something happens.

Everything fades away. Suddenly there is no Abba, no moon, just a void. She has no arms, legs, head, neck or hands. She senses a fluttering where her legs are meant to be, looking down, she sees *a tail with paper streamers*. She is no longer herself.

She has become a kite careening into a vortex...

* * * * * *

The beige bedroom is cool and comfortable when she wakes up. The smell of *motia* wafts through as the air conditioner spreads the fragrance of the chains of flowers hanging over its vents. She looks over at the nightstand; her clock says it is 3:20 in large, glowing, red numbers. Her ivory silk nightie has ridden up. She pulls it down as she sits up against the large, white satin padded headboard, reaching for the red and gold Dunhill cigarette packet.

She gingerly pulls one out with her long, pearl pink fingernails and lights it with a lighter that snaps open into flame and just as quickly snaps shut. She walks over to the window and looks out into the garden. Over her shoulder she glances back at the white bed and views the empty space in the bed next to hers. He is not back yet. Why would he be? What did it matter?

She knows exactly where he is. Sitting at one of his crony's houses, he is drinking Black Label in a tumbler in which the ice never seems to melt, smoking Monte Cristos and gambling his inherited *crores* into the night.

On the wall next to the window is an array of wedding photographs, in varying sizes, of her in differing staged poses, in the studio and at the wedding functions — wearing her array of many bridal costumes. There's the one where she is looking down at the ground demurely as all good Pakistani brides were supposed to, her heavily embroidered *dupatta* dyed in a melody of pastel pink and earth tones, placed just so on her head.

There's the one where she is looking *into* the camera, her heavily hennaed hand holding the edge of her *dupatta* in a carefully crafted Bollywood-inspired pose.

There's the one of her sitting in a chair, her long, voluminous skirt fanned out. He is standing behind her in his white raw silk sherwani and pajama, a hand on her shoulder — the ceremonial golden brocade *pagri* on his head, disproportionate to everything else in the photo.

'Had there been even one real thing about the wedding?' she wonders. 'Just one?' Perhaps, she thinks, she is being too hard on herself. After all, there was never anything real at these highly staged weddings — just pomp and circumstance. No utterance of vows or exchange of emotion. No 'now you may kiss the bride.' No public display of love between the bride and groom on an occasion supposedly to celebrate love.

She remembers an array of photographs being clicked of her and Anjum. She remembers a never-ending parade of unrecognizable people coming up to her on the stage and greeting her, kissing her, congratulating her. She had smiled, and smiled and smiled and smiled some more.

Well she had been happy; thrilled to bits in fact. And her mother had been ecstatic. In fact, she mused there was no happier person at the wedding than her mother standing on the platform proud and triumphant like a Roman conqueress who had just annexed a vast kingdom.

Wait, yes there had been something real. Ami Jaan had clambered onto the stage held her head in both her rough hands, kissed her on the forehead and said:

'*Jeeti raho beti*. Live on and on my daughter.' Then she had sat next to her through the many hours of pageantry, with a calming hand resting lightly on Rumina's knee.

By that time, she recalled — she, Rumina, had managed to deceive everyone. Her act had been so complete, so perfect that she had fooled even herself, and once that had happened fooling everyone else was a doddle. Even Ami Jaan believed that she was truly happy, too old by then to pare through the layers with her razor-sharp acumen, and too good a person to question her granddaughter's motives for marrying.

As she stares out of the window, she sees it all. Her

life flashing before her eyes as they say it does when you are about to die. Yet she knew she was not about to die, for she was already dead. How simple it had all seemed at the time. The turning point had come really, when shortly after her nineteenth birthday, Durriya Dadabhoy had extended an invitation to her mother and her to attend a farmhouse musical evening.

She recalls that at the time there could have been no better reward for her mother. All the days and nights manoeuvring like a general deploying his troops strategically in order to affect a greater victory had finally paid off. 'Why had her mother been so hungry for her sake?' she wonders. After all Abba was a perfectly good man, had she not been happy with him? He had done everything for her, showered her with affection and as much material wealth as he could afford. 'Why was someone like Abba just not good enough for her daughter?'

She waited for answers to come to her but none were forthcoming on the night breeze as the leaves of the *jamun* trees rustled.

All fingers pointed towards her, and she knew this.

2

A Glut Of Skin

In preparation for the farmhouse musical evening, Rumina had spent the whole day at the salon. Julie, Salma and Angie fussed and fretted over her as if she were a bride getting ready for the big day.

They had charted her and her mother's progress over the years and were the cheerleaders to their game of social football. Not that they were privy to all the details of the plays created by her mother the coach — they were, however, given small morsels of information by Rana Shaukat Khan strategically — such that they would both enjoy and possibly leak to other teams and other coaches to the advantage of Team Guddi, ensuring a healthy supply of juicy tips.

On this day Rumina had the works. She started with the skin-whitening facial to allow her face time to recover if there were any unsightly blotches or inflammation. Then Angie waxed her entire body. Each nail at the end of each finger and toe on each hand and foot was cleaned, pressed, massaged, filed, buffed and polished while Rumina dreamt languorously of how beautiful she would look. Her mother sat by the whole time making sure everything was done right.

'No Salma, shape the nails squareish not round. These days square is in fashion. No, not red nail polish — a pinkish tinge will be better.'

As she sat with her eyes closed whilst Julie massaged her feet and legs with almond oil, Rumina could hear the roar of blow driers, the clattering of tea cups on counters, and the urgent hum and murmur of chatting women punctuated with the occasional laugh. As she drifted away, she saw the palm trees lining sparkling boulevards, and there she was at the wheel of a red convertible, her hair blowing in the pure California air.

The sound of the hair driers became the rush of the cars on the road. In her reverie, she wore a diminutive strappy top, her hands on the wheel. She was complete in her freedom and her control.

'All done *baji*', Julie said. Rumina opened her eyes, just as she had reached the ocean. The lights appeared brighter in the salon. She smiled and stretched.

'You fell asleep!' Salma busy at her mother's feet exclaimed.

'It must be all the excitement,' her mother said, 'The poor thing is exhausted. Shopping, facial, waxing!' Indeed, when her mother said that Rumina did feel more than a little tired.

It had taken whole three weeks of shopping to find the right outfit, jewellry, shoes and handbag, which entailed going to a thousand shops a day to find just the right thing at just the right price. No purchases could occur without haggling and comparison shopping. At first, they had thought they would get something stitched, so there were about three days of fabric shopping. But then Rumina saw the most spectacular outfit at Devanand Pritesh, the only Hindu designer to have ever broken through in Pakistan, and pined after it until her mother gave in.

It cost 68,000 rupees but it was perfect; a marvel of black chiffon and subtle yet substantial embroidery. The clincher was that it was similar to the outfit that Topsy Raja, who Rumina secretly worshipped as her role model, had worn to her own brother's wedding.

Whilst everyone else wore colours, Topsy had chosen black. It was an immaculate Riaz Babar sari that had all the Aunties gasping at the glut of Topsy's beautiful creamy skin it exposed in the arms, back, waist, stomach and neckline. Rumina thought Topsy had looked like a maharani, and she dreamt of someday having the nerve and abandon of the upper classes to make an entrance like that.

Only recently had Rumina started tentatively wearing sleeveless apparel. The pressure to conform to the hip and trendy had been too great to fight. Sleeveless clothing had become the badge of the liberal, emancipated but fashion-conscious woman. Karachi was a sweltering city most of the year so it made sense for women to abandon their sleeves, but it took generations of sleeve-wearing women for the patriarchy to be able to allow for it — just about.

At first the phenomenon was only seen at private parties. Then some women took it to the streets in broad daylight. The majority were still very much ensleeved, and would remain so, but for those who had made it their own — it was the only way to dress in the hot Karachi sun. Rumina was amongst those women for whom the vision of their arms was one only a select few were privy to. These women kept it to private functions, never in the daytime in public.

So the 'avante' style of sari blouse, not much more than a glorified handkerchief that Topsy had sported, was not something Rumina would ever wear. But a girl could dream. Her new black outfit and Topsy's outfit were related only in spirit. Rumina's was a chiffon black sleeveless *kameez* with a deep but not explicit neckline — it was the diamond-shaped cut-out on the back that she felt was more 'her' — subtle exposure.

Silver embroidery adorned the extremities giving it

the expensive touch. It was the trousers that were a truly novel thing for Rumina. They were cropped and so flashed a little leg which was the new advancement in the *shalwar*; higher and more streamlined. Gone were the days of the baggy shalwar coming in narrow at the ankles. Now it was all narrow and no bag — 'pant *shalwar*'.

The shoes were high, airy and silver. The matched purse an elegant, bejewelled hard-case shell with a belcher chain strap.

'Ready for hair now?' asked Julie, herding Rumina towards the hair salon area. 'What should I do Amma?' Rumina asked feeling lost and uncertain in that moment. Rana Khan however, knew exactly where she was and exactly what she wanted.

'I think you should blow dry it and put it up *jaani*. You know like with a strand in front of your face?'

'*Haan*. Yes, yes,' Julie and Salma bobbed their heads in unison, 'that will look very nice!'

3

Greener Pastures

The first time they met, she recalls with no real amazement, there were no bells going off, nor were there whistles. In fact, she had thought Anjum *rather ugly*. He came up to her after the musical evening whilst she was getting a 7-Up from the drinks table.

'So — you must be Rumina,' he said in a deep but manicured voice. Turning around she saw a man in a crisp expensive-looking white shirt with one too many buttons open, displaying a black carpet of chest hair. He wore a garish gold watch and an even more garish gold ring. Her mother's classic words had entered her head '... darker than your father.' Yes — this man had in fact been a candidate for her mother's favourite measure of dark skin. He had had nice hair, yes.

As she stands in her room, many years later, her nightie fluttering in the breeze from the air conditioner on this long, dark night of the soul, she is comforted by the fact that she had thought he had nice hair; thick and wavy. There had been a brutish, raw sensuality to him. She had smiled sweetly and not said much, letting him do most of the talking.

'So, are you enjoying the musical evening?' he had asked.

'Yes, but I haven't really attended any others!'

'You haven't?' he seemed shocked.

'No.'

'Well,' he laughed, 'you haven't missed much. They're deathly dull!' She laughed in turn.

'Well it was nice to meet you,' he said upon taking his leave. As it turned out, Anjum Dadabhoy was the eldest son, well-known for his playboy extravagance and flamboyant lifestyle. His younger brothers were already married, and his mother had now issued him an ultimatum.

He was getting married, and *she* was finding him the girl. Durriya wanted to find someone 'sober,' who may actually *reform* her son; she *knew* another typical society-type would not help *her* in *her* goal for her son. Or so Mrs. Kazmi had told Mrs. Akram who had told Rumina's mother. As they sat around drinking coffee, post-farmhouse-musical-evening, Mrs. Akram said she had it on good authority that Durriya had her eye on Rumina for Anjum.

'I'm telling you Rana. It's only a matter of time!'

'Isn't she looking at other girls too?'

'*Haan* — yes she must be — but she wouldn't have invited you to her farmhouse if Rumina was not on her mind.'

Rana had felt her heart lurch, lost in her personal fantasies of the dream society wedding for her daughter Mrs. Akram continued talking.

'And you know he is quite a catch. Not only are they wealthy but he has studied in America, lived there for a long time and all the sons have foreign passports you know!' Rana Shaukat caught the last part snapping her head around to listen more carefully, 'Really?' she asked — well-shaped eyebrows climbing higher up her face.

'Yes, Yes. The younger brother Imran got married and moved to New York last year. So nice for the girl!'

'What!' Rumina had been overjoyed when her mother

had returned with this morsel of information. Overnight, Anjum had appeared much more handsome in her mind. So what if the hair on his hands was as thick as his chest hair. So what if his pants were just a little too tight, and yes he was a little older than she would have liked him to be, but none of that mattered so much if there was a chance that she would leave Karachi, leave Pakistan for beachy pastures.

'Anyway *beta,*' her mother had cautioned, 'please don't get too excited yet. Apparently, Durriya is also considering other girls for him.' From then on, however, Rumina could think of nothing else. This had to happen. It would happen. She knew it in her bones and perhaps, she realized later, willed it into being.

* 4 *

Trussed & Trustability

Her Pasha white marble house in Defence Phase 5 had slowly become a cage, and she was the nightingale in this gilded prison. How could she have been so superficial? After discovering what Anjum had to offer, Rumina had redoubled efforts to become his wife.

She made sure she met all the people she knew who knew him, in order to get closer to him, dropping hints and telling tales hoping they would get back to him. She heard about his reputation and even came across the women whose hearts he had broken but was unconcerned. She would change all that. She heard from his cousin's friend who was the sister of a friend of Rumina's from college that he and his mother were fighting and that it was she who was forcing marriage on him, but there was apparently, 'one girl' who had tickled his fancy.

'I think it's you Rummi!' the younger sister of her friend had told her.

'How do you know that?'

'Because Aunty Durryia told my mother,' said the young unsuspecting informant, her eyes sparkling at the joy of being a part of the intrigue.

She met him a few times before they got married. There had been a few strategic events designed for the express purpose of the 'boy' and 'girl' getting to know each other a little. There were always others involved. She had noticed he consistently had a crystal tumbler of scotch clasped firmly in his hand, but was always well-behaved. Like most scions to a family fortune he talked a great deal about himself; his money, his father's 'business'. It was never clear to Rumina what exactly this 'business' was or what Anjum actually did, but he said he would go to the 'factory' or the 'site'. Textiles were mentioned, so was sugar, or was it cement, she couldn't be sure.

Eventually he called her up at home and invited her to come out to dinner with him. Rumina had never been more nervous. She had not been at such close quarters with a man, especially not one she may be spending the rest of her life with. They had gone to the Thai restaurant in Pearl Continental where they allowed you to bring your own alcohol and served it to you surreptitiously in a teapot.

He poured her red wine and seemed quite stunned when she said she didn't drink.

'Really?'

'Yes, really,' she replied gently to which he repeated:

'Really?' smiling slyly.

'Come on!' Rumina had seen the potential for a new avenue to open up in her life, but she was clear that that particular evening was not the time for it.

Dinner had been slightly more revealing than her public social interactions with him, yet he gave nothing away. There was no talk of marriage or engagement or anything so uncivilized. He would not do his own dirty work, all would be arranged and taken care of — and Rumina too was relieved not to have the pressure of that on their interactions.

He talked a little of America and told Rumina that he 'wouldn't mind returning there one day,' and then had added, 'maybe when I'm married you know?' He made this sound like a very off-hand comment. But she knew it was intended to make him more desirable.

The game wasn't just played one way, after all. Men, too were trussed up and basted like turkeys at Christmas for the marriage market, perhaps not in the same way or to the same extent, but it did occur. Rumina was flattered that he thought he needed to make himself more attractive to her, and was jubilant that this was in fact a possibility.

It was that night, that she revealed to him, a more truthful version of herself, 'I've always wanted to go to California,' she said coyly not daring to look at him. He was bobbing his head in positive agreement, not quite listening.

'Yeah it's great there!' he threw out off-handedly.

She had wondered then exactly which version of her history and story he and his mother knew, and how much of it. They obviously thought she was a suitable match in terms of stature, but how many lies would she have to cover up? And how would she if they were married?

5

Sohaag Raat:
Wedding Night

She soon learned that none of her or her mother's lies mattered. No-one really cared about her. As long she looked the part and acted the part no-one would be checking up on her. Her father had enough money saved to give her a lavish wedding. And once she was installed with her in-laws what did it matter? It was a new life, and hopefully she thought in those days of nuptial preparation — her new life would continue in America, in California — in Melrose Place! That's what had really kept her going.

She thought of nothing else, and her mother didn't help. She filled her head with all sorts of fantasies of what happened to the wives of 'foreign passport holders'. Topsy had married Jawad, and he applied for a spousal passport and she got it within a few months and they had gone off to London! Raza and Bina; Saima and Afzal; the list went on and on. None of the information was complete or even accurate, for that matter, Rumina mused — sitting down heavily on the white leather sofa in her bedroom, reaching for the bottle of red wine she had opened earlier — drinking till she fell asleep.

What her mother hadn't known were the stipulations that went with immigration. What a difference it made depending on if the boy had actually lived in the country of which he was a national for the last few years, or how much it cost to apply for these things, or even how many stages there were till the couples she had mentioned actually got to that point where they were standing in a queue at the airport luggage and all.

However, the mothers had had many talks and Durriya had pretty much made Rana believe that Rumina could well find herself sitting in London or New York.

'We have a flat in Kensington you know,' Durriya told Rana.

'And his father and I have been trying to get Anjum to go and spend some time in London to help his father's business contacts. Let's see?' she said taking a well-timed sip from her delicate china teacup.

'Maybe your daughter can convince him?' she added placing the teacup back on the table with a knowing smile. On another occasion she told Rana Shaukat about Anjum's uncle who lived in New York and wanted his nephew to come and help him with his lucrative consultancy firm.

'I'm telling you *beta* you are as good as gone!' Rana had told her daughter, and then in a rare show of emotion said, 'but then what will I do? Once you're gone?'

Rumina looked at her mother, shocked at this show of emotion — her expression puppy-like. She went to put her arms around her mother's shoulders.

'Oh Amma! Don't worry — I'm sure you'll keep yourself busy! And then of course you will be visiting me for months on end, no? And helping me set up a new house.'

Rana perked up considerably envisioning herself, striding purposefully down the streets of London and New York — lording it over decorators, painters, and handymen whilst trying to get her daughter's house abroad set up. She could finally visit Harrods, K-nightsbridge and that Oxx-Ford Street!

'God what a joke my mother is' — thinks Rumina as

she pours herself a glass wine, cupping the rounded base in the palm of her hand.

Her wedding night had been a disaster. After the parade of friends and family had left them alone in their hotel room — after the obligatory rituals of barring entry to the groom, after the girl's side extracted money from him for *all* the members of the posse *after* hiding his shoe — they had sat, her on the sofa, him on the bed staring at each other for a while.

'You look very beautiful,' he said. As he got closer and sat by her side she was struck by his breath. It smelt like he had pickled his tongue in alcohol, but she was too nervous to say anything, merely turning her face away ever so slightly.

She had been told how to sit when it came to this; looking down and not saying anything.

'You just have to let the guy do whatever he wants to!' her elder cousin Shama Apa had imparted to her in a god-awful conversation (that her mother had obviously requested her to have with Rumina — too embarrassed to have it herself).

And so she had sat there not saying anything — not even daring to look up at her new husband. Anjum had gotten bored with this and stood up to face her lifting her chin up with his hand. That night she had gotten a good look at him for the first time.

His hair was slicked back and his hairline which was receding a little — was prominent and boasted a perfectly formed peak. She had thought he looked moderately handsome in his off-white raw silk *sherwani*. But now — two and a half years on — she recalls instead how the high, narrow collar of the attire made his neck look thick and cruel.

'So are you going to say anything?' he had asked 'Or are you going to keep up this 'traditional bride' act?' Rumina shivers as she recalls him saying those words just as she had felt the chill run through her when he had said them.

'What act?' She was putting on no act. This is how brides were supposed to behave! She had looked at him askance. He had not spoken spitefully, and he had a sly smile on his face.

She wonders, as she feels the wine going down her throat, warming her chest and then her stomach, where she had found the courage to say what she had said next, 'What would you like me to 'act' like?'

'I don't want you to 'act'. Be yourself. Who are you in there?'

'I think you know who I am. You've married me.'

'Yeah but we don't know each other at all. Isn't it weird?'

'Weird?' She had been puzzled by him.

'I think you're drunk,' she had finally said.

'Well of course I'm drunk! It's my wedding day, and you should be drunk too!'

'I told you I don't drink.'

He had walked across the room and opened a bag that was lying on the dressing table — extracting a bottle of champagne and two delicate crystal glasses that glinted like her new diamonds. With a grand gesture he had pulled the cork. It had given itself up with a pleasant sounding 'pop' and he had poured the gently fizzing light pink liquid.

'You do now baby! Pink champagne!'

Apa had said to do whatever he wanted, so she took the glass from him and followed his lead. He had made a toast.

'To you! Mrs Anjum!' He told her champagne was supposed to be sipped, but she took a huge gulp, and so they gulped and sipped and gulped their way through three bottles of champagne. She laughed a great deal and it made the whole thing a lot less nerve-wracking. He had found her first-time drunkenness endearing.

Somehow her clothes came off. He had taken them off as she giggled. Seeing him naked for the first time had been a shock, she remembers that. He had so much hair on his body she thought he looked like a grizzly bear. They had kissed and she hoped she was doing it right. When he put his tongue in her mouth, she did the same. When he stroked her back, she stroked his back.

After the marriage was finally consummated she remembers feeling lost. But if there was pain like her friends and Apa had warned her of — she may have been safely numbed to it by the pink bubbles. At one point his weight on top of her had alarmed her, some — she had felt like she was suffocating.

Her gasp had prompted him to look up at her, and she would never forgot the look in his eyes. It had seemed like he was far, far away, in a fog. It hadn't even seemed like he recognized her.

There was another thing she never forgot. He had taken a name 'Uzma', just after he had rolled off her before falling asleep immediately. Even in her inebriated state she knew she had heard right and remembered being confused for the few seconds before she too passed out.

He had been sweet the next morning though. She hadn't known why her head was so heavy. He had known and laughed at her, kissing her on the forehead.

'You my dear have a First Class Hangover. Nothing major since you drank only the best champagne,' he had said winking at her. In the light of day with his body exposed he looked like a jovial giant, the skin matted with hair, warm and inviting. He had gotten out of bed to get her a glass of water. She had cringed with embarrassment at seeing his buttocks exposed, and herself lay clutching the sheet tightly over her body.

'Thank you Anjum,' she said gingerly sipping the water in a way that did not expose her too much.

Anjum had immediately picked up on her shyness. He got back into the bed and within minutes his hands were on her breasts. She had shrieked. He had laughed some more. 'Well you're going to have to get used to this you know.'

She had blushed, furiously clutching the sheet around her. He had not stopped and pretty soon he was making love to her. This had been different, terrifying, and more real than the night before.

She tried not to move too much because she thought that was probably what she was supposed to do. She kept closing her eyes but didn't want him to think she didn't want to look at him. She noticed that he had his eyes closed most of the time and so just let go.

It hadn't lasted very long — and afterwards they had fallen asleep again — her curled up against him — him with his arms sprawled over his head, snoring gently.

* * * * * *

Now nearly three years on, it is a rare occasion when he actually even sleeps in the bed with her at the same time. She lights another cigarette, inhales deeply and as she releases the smoke wonders what it would have been like had she taken Ami Jaan's advice and actually married someone she loved.

She was ashamed. Ashamed of her mother, ashamed of herself. Why hadn't she ever had more nerve? Like Rabia who was now working in television and was married to a guy she really loved — that she had found *herself*.

She missed Kiran and Rabia and all her friends who were not sycophants and cloying socialites. Rumina was tired of the same old thing day after day, night after night. She had started to see the rich and powerful women she met up with almost every day — tedious and shallow.

She was bored of shopping and discussing the latest Chanel shades or the latest Mulberry bag. There had to be more to life. She knew there was. Her mother drove her nuts, still exactly the same. Except now the pressure was on her to enter the baby-making competition. Rana Shaukat Khan constantly regaled her with stories of which Mrs Whatever's daughter or daughter-in-law had had what child, at what hospital and what gifts she had received.

This was a moot point with Rumina. There was one thing she had taken a stand on. She would not give into her mother or Durriya Dadabhoy's pressure to procreate. Her marriage to Anjum had been like a business transaction — she thinks bitterly. She knew that now, but neither party had fulfilled their end of the unspoken contract.

* 6 *

Pleasure & Forgetting

There were parties. So many parties. Nothing but. Rumina spent the first few years of marriage in a whirlwind. She could buy whatever she wanted, whenever she wanted. Anjum was extravagant, flamboyant, and she soon learnt that he wanted his wife to be the same. He often refused to go out with her if she wasn't dressed in a way that pleased him. That almost always involved her showing more skin.

'Anjum what kind of man are you?' she asked in anger, 'why do you want your wife on display?'

'I can't be seen with you if you look like a girl from the village!' He often said things like that.

'Village? What village? Just because I don't dress like those tarts that are always hanging all over you doesn't mean I'm from a 'village'!'

He slowly picked at her sense of self-worth making her feel inadequate and cheapened by his desire to put her on display. Initially, there were many nights that he would not take her with him and she was left alone feeling hurt and lost. The advice she always got from other women was the same, 'Just do whatever he wants.'

Eventually, a heart rankling with resentment, as she trawled the boutiques and made endless trips to tailors, she modified the way she dressed — like a very slow strip tease — revealing body parts over time.

She tried her best to fit in at these parties. But despite her best efforts everyone always appeared rather more glamorous, had much more to say and were much more exciting than her.

She had spent a great deal of her older teenage years trying to get to this point where she too would be communing with the rich and powerful, but now she just found them rich and tedious. Anjum often left her in the lurch to fend for herself amongst the wolves.

After their wedding night she had not succumbed to Anjum's pressure to drink again for a long time. The unending rigour of social events where she was the only teetotaller had eventually changed her mind. It fit the golden rule after all, '*Just do whatever he wants you to do.*'

With drinking, Rumina almost believed life got better. She too now talked loudly, laughed loudly and was excited to meet people like each one was a long-lost friend. Anjum seemed much more at ease with this new Rumina, too. He still left her to canoodle with friends that he didn't introduce her to at parties. But more time elapsed between the time they would arrive and he would disappear.

He seemed more affectionate. Squeezing a shoulder — a kiss on the cheek, putting his arm around her — she recalls actually having some falsely formed perception of feeling for him, at the time.

They laughed together, he got her to dance more — the alcohol giving her the bravado to try. The only dancing she had done previously was the traditional kind at weddings to impress the Grand Dames of Karachi — in order to interest them in her for their sons. In fact, maybe Durriya had seen just one such performance when Rumina caught her eye for Anjum.

They often ended up at the beach at 4 or 5 in the morning at someone's, 'hut'. Anjum too had a 'hut' at French

Beach, which Rumina had been extremely impressed with the first time she saw it. It was like a house in Defence only on the ocean front in a secluded spot. It was equipped with everything that was needed for perfect days and nights at the beach — electricity generators to rest unencumbered by the perpetual power outages, hot water, a working kitchen, plenty of rooms for inebriated revellers to crash or, as she discovered, for couples to get intimate.

Rumina was shocked at how much more relaxed and open the subject of sex was in the new social world she inhabited. It was almost as if everyone was restricted and conservative until they managed to hit the big time. And then all the rules changed. It was as if it was no longer the same country. It was a world where money seemed to buy everything, including the illusion of freedom.

The have-nots dreamt of a Pakistan that had the trappings of the Western world such as they saw in on their satellite dishes in Western films and on television, whilst the haves just created it. There may not be bars, clubs or other public social spaces where men and women could meet and interact — but in the elite echelons there were parties, balls, galas, dinners, casino nights so that they never actually lived by the laws of the land.

Whereas alcohol was unavailable to most (unless they knew someone who knew someone and then only if they had 600 rupees to spare for one beer) — for the upper classes it was magically easy to procure.

It flowed at parties, all imported, all legal within the confines of their palatial homes. These nights were the mirages in the desert. In these mirages there was no oppressive fundamentalist religion governing the actions of people, no awareness of the level of corruption in successive governments

— just a shared desire for pleasure and forgetting.

* 7 *

Mr. Guddi

Whenever she saw a couple locked in passion in full view at a party, she did her best not to stare, but it was a struggle — like being unable to look away from a car crash. She was fascinated and flabbergasted, but could not share these feelings with anybody. She knew Anjum would find her provincial. At one such moment at a party, she heard a deep voice next to her, 'Yeah it's crazy isn't it? I am a good middle-class boy and for me this is shocking!'

Looking around startled, she saw a good-natured face grinning at her.

'What?' she said.

'It's ok. I know what you're thinking' he said confidently.

'How could you know what I was thinking?'

'I can tell by your face, you're not one of these people,' he said mysteriously, making her blush and look at her feet.

'Your eyes aren't glazed over with boredom and your mouth isn't set in a permanent scowl.'

'Is that what you think of 'these people'?' she asked.

'Well isn't that what you think?'

'I really don't see how that's any of your business,' she said flustered and walked off to the French doors leading into the garden where Anjum was by the bar.

'Hey babe! Need a drink?'

'Yes, go on,' said Rumina.

'A drink for my wife!' Anjum announced, his voice booming. Many hands rushed to get her a drink. One finally handed her a glass of champagne. She raised the flute to her lips and when she removed it, she caught sight of her mystery man talking to a few people in the opposite corner of the party.

He caught sight of her and without missing a beat made a mock salute that made her chortle into her champagne. Anjum didn't notice as he was busy talking over everyone else heatedly about some polo-related issue.

She had never seen this guy before. He did seem a little out-of-place. He didn't look as shiny and plastic. He looked a little more substantial, his hair was not immaculate — he wasn't sporting any bling — but what she noticed most was that out of everyone else present, he seemed the most at ease — with himself and with everyone else.

* * * * * *

'Anjum, where are you going?'

'I'll be back babe. Look there's Bibo why don't you go say hello?' He grabbed her arm not violently but with emphasis and led her over to where a few women were conversing.

The tallest of them had bronzed glowing skin, and cheekbones that could carve wood. Her hair was slicked back like an oiled horse's mane shiny and black. Her outfit was Grecian with one shoulder bared and the other draped loosely with white flowing fabric that continued its journey down her body gracefully in a rhapsody of folds tapering at her ankles.

When she saw the couple approaching — she shrieked,

'Anjuuuummm Darrrling! Ruuummmi!' She was a harmless enough character — a model who was stunningly beautiful and glamorous with no pretension whatsoever. From her very first meeting with Rumina she had been loving and caring. She was related to the family in some way Rumina didn't fully understand but that was always the case in Pakistan. Everyone was related somehow — some said it was from all the inter-cousin marriages.

'You look darrrling Ruuuumi!' she enthused. This was one of the nights Rumina had felt extra brave. She had donned a strappy shirt that was fitted at the waist and bust, and her elegant trousers were almost up to her knees. She had taken a page out of the Karachi models and had slicked her hair back into an elegant chignon. The whole outfit was a deep, blood red and she had been relieved when Anjum had approved, 'Sexy baby,' he said, making her blush.

Despite Bibo's protests that he stay and talk to her — Anjum managed to extricate himself having deposited Rumina in five seconds flat. Bibo smiled and shook her head, 'I hope he's behaving himself,' to which Rumina just smiled politely and shook her head.

'You know he is a good guy. He's just too used to being alone and doing whatever he wants. You really have to tame him *jaani*!'

'Tame him?' Rumina could not imagine that was possible, or maybe she just wasn't too bothered. Let him do whatever he wanted she thought, just as long as soon they would be out of here — to America or London.

To Bibo, Rumina said nothing — politely agreeing with her. She liked Bibo who was always nice to her, but there was no point exchanging confidences. She had learnt to keep her mouth firmly shut in matters of her marriage. Word just spread too fast, about everything — most often distorted beyond recognition and Bibo was a well-known blabbermouth — not so much a malicious gossip, but someone who was unable to keep anything in.

'Guddi?' Rumina swivelled around upon hearing a familiar voice call her by that name, 'Kiran?'

'Oh my god! It is you!' Kiran rushed to give Rumina a hug.

They had not met since Rumina's wedding as Kiran had moved to Lahore to attend N.C.A., the prestigious arts college.

'Kiran what are you doing here?' Rumina could not believe she was seeing her dear old friend in this sea of strangers. She remembers experiencing a huge sense of relief, such that she had not in a long time.

'I'm getting married! I came back to start the preparations, and it so happens that the guy I am marrying is related to the couple who are hosting this party!'

'What! How exciting! Mubarik to you! You have to tell me everything!'

'I will, I will,' said Kiran excitedly, 'Guddi I nearly didn't recognize you *yaar*. *Uff* how amazing you look!'

'Don't be silly I look the same.'

'If you say so. I've never seen you look so... so... trendy!' They both grinned at each other, and for a brief moment they were transported to their days in college together.

'Sooo — where's Mr. Guddi?'

'First you tell me where this lucky man who is your

fiancé is!'

The re-entrance of Kiran into her life had been a turning point. That night Rumina had felt as close to being herself as possible. They remained attached at the hip all night; Kiran introducing Rumina to people from her artsy group of friends and Rumina introducing her to her society friends.

Anjum had been more boisterous than usual, welcoming Kiran with a big hug. He of course, knew the guy she was marrying — Salman, and gave his seal of approval. Salman was an industrialist's son who had rebelled against the family by not taking his place in the family business and gone to attend art school (where he and Kiran had met). His parents had previously thought their son was gay and had openly lamented the fact.

'Yeah man, his parents are a bit too narrow-minded. But now he has the last laugh because he's a really famous photographer and he's started his own business. Of course — I'm sure the family contacts did help, between you and me!' Kiran had told her.

Rumina was re-invigorated by Kiran's stories. It was all so exciting. Like her husband-to-be, she had done well at the National College Of Arts and was an up and coming fashion designer. Rumina had put on her best brave face for Kiran pretending she was happy too.

There was no way she would let her in to meet her inner demons. She had a companion at the social events now and had thrown herself into helping Kiran prepare for her upcoming marriage with gusto.

8

Nose Candy

Casino night took place once a month in rotation at only the most influential families' homes. Anjum hosted them from time to time as well. That night they had set out for his close friend who they all called 'Johnny's' mansion in Old Clifton.

Rumina detested Casino nights most of all. She wasn't interested in participating and neither was Anjum interested in having her participate but she had to be there — all the guys had to have their women there to make the night complete, like cheerleaders at a football game.

She, however, unlike the other women couldn't bear to stand there hanging over Anjum faux-squealing at his wins and faux-lamenting his losses. Most nights she had the driver take her home once Anjum was too involved (and too drunk) to notice.

That night, the gates of Johnny's mansion, slid open after a honk from their car and their driver greeted the guard with a muted nod. As they drove slowly up the extensive driveway, it was like being in a small city. There were houses behind houses for the joint families to live in privacy. Palm trees lining the driveway swayed in the warm, fragrant night breeze.

Up ahead glamour was oozing out of the parking cars. Rumina took a quiet, sharp inward breath — bracing herself for a night of polite, empty conversation. Kiran had said she might be there with her fiance but was not sure because it really wasn't his scene — even though he had grown up with these people. Rumina pleaded her case and had requested that Kiran do her best to convince her fiancé Salman, because she needed the company.

In the main area all the gambling tables were set up in neat rows on either side of the grand room, with the dealer neatly suited and booted in a black bow-tie and black waistcoat stationed at the head. There was a mixed bag of people, as these events tended to bring out the legendary older socialites who had partied in Karachi in the 70s, when there was cabaret, jazz and a massive casino in Clifton built by the optimistic but misguided Zulfiqar Ali Bhutto.

The tang of cigar smoke filled the air, looming in blue circles above the tables. The men wore formal suits and the women were more elaborate than usual — clutching gilded purses in one hand and a glass in the other. Rumina would never get used to this side of Karachi; it was totally and utterly foreign to her, but Anjum had grown up in it.

As a child he watched his father, father's friends and uncles at it, as a teenager him and his friends were at it, and today Anjum, his friends, his father's friends, his father and uncles were all at it, together.

In the early days of her marriage she had spoken to her mother about it, 'But Amma these people gamble!'

'So what if they gamble? Let them gamble. What goes of your father? This is their right *beta*.'

'But Amma I hate it! It's so boring!'

'Well you're his wife if anyone can make him stop, it would be you. Your father used to love playing chess with his friends and I made him stop. They used to play all night like hooligans.' Rumina laughed. She never knew this secret life of her father, and imagined him dashing and young — scowling over a chess board.

'He was even the Sargodha Chess Champion in his teenage days!'

'Wow Amma. Why did you make him stop?'

'Because! He was a married man and had a wife and a child to attend to. You can't do these types of things forever you know.' What a restrictive world-view her mother had Rumina thought. Why could you not do the *something you loved* forever? She felt bad for her father and the loss of his beloved chess playing.

'Drink, madam?' A bearer in a white suit with a burgundy bow-tie & *pagri* on his head, offered her a flute from the tray he was balancing deftly on one hand. Why not, she thought, better now than later. She joined the smiling–and–sipping party — as Anjum installed himself at the blackjack table, his friends loudly cheering. Out of the window, she noticed the leaves of the banana trees in the garden outside swaying, and the bougainvillea lit up by the garden lights glowing magenta.

'Eh Guddi!' Kiran had arrived after all and Rumina clutched onto her.

'Easy, easy — I'm sure it isn't that bad!' her friend quipped.

'Look around you Kir. It is! Where's Salman?'

'Oh — you know he's trying to entertain himself. He figures these parties are probably good for his art.'

'So — he's not into the gambling at all?'

'No way *yaar*,' Kiran replied screwing up her nose as if she had smelt something bad. It had been a few hours since Rumina had arrived. She noticed Anjum was not at the table anymore and neither were his friends. Maybe he had gone outside to meet someone.

'Where's the HUBBY *this* evening?' Kiran asked.

'Well he *was* over there,' Rumina pointed.

'Right,' Kiran rolled her eyes and tapped her nose knowingly, 'He's probably gone for a little refreshment!'

'What do you mean?'

Kiran was alarmed by the genuine incomprehension on Rumina's face, '*You know* — Guddi!' Kiran tried to blag it, hoping her old friend was not as naive as she appeared.

'No — I don't know, Kiran.'

'You mean you really don't know?'

'Really don't know what, Kiran?'

'Come here,' gestured Kiran taking Rumina's arm and taking her outside.

Rumina was engulfed by the sweet night air which calmed her. There was nothing so bad, she realized that she couldn't hear. Kiran and her walked onto the grass arm in arm.

'So?' she asked Kiran.

'Guddi you are just such a lost lamb *yaar*. Don't you know what these jet-sets get up to? Well that is to say... your husband and his friends? They're doing cocaine *yaar!*'

'Cocaine?' Rumina echoed not so much questioning as repeating it back to verify.

'Yah Co-cai-ne,' Kiran repeated making a gesture with her finger to her nostril — moving her head up and down.

'But how do you know for sure?'

'Well *jaan*, it's pretty obvious, but actually Salman's cousin who is related to Anjum's buddy Nomi mentioned it. I didn't think much of it to be honest. I mean everyone does it now.'

'Really?'

'Guddi you are ok, right?' Rumina said nothing for a moment. Yes — she was alright actually.

'Is that why he's so over-excited when I see him after he's disappeared at these parties?' She asked Kiran, genuinely interested to which she replied, 'Yah probably!'

Just then they caught sight of Anjum — now on the other side of the window. He was surrounded by his friends, his head thrown back in uproarious laughter. Rumina started giggling.

'What's so funny?' Kiran asked a little worried.

'Look at him,' Rumina said,

'Just- look- at- him,' her voice tearing a little.

9

Daybreak

In the distance, pye-dogs are barking up a storm. Rumina has now finished the bottle of beaujolais. It was the only red the bootlegger had had apparently, when she sent the driver off to purchase her bi-monthly cases.

It hasn't been that long since she discovered Anjum's cocaine habit. She knows it is widening the gulf between them. She didn't bother confronting him, there was no point. The day after that, however, she did decide to speak to Anjum about her American passport again. He had kept saying he would do it, but she didn't think he had as yet. She hadn't wanted to seem too eager and so had tried not to nag. After Kiran's revelation to her though — she felt it imperative to know.

Anjum usually awoke at 3 or 4 in the afternoon. The earliest she had ever seen him wake was 11:30, which happened whenever his father gave him hell — occurring every six months or so — or of course, on Beach Sundays, when the two plus hour drive necessitated it. When he was dragged into office, Anjum would moderately alter his behaviour for all of a few days and then slide back to his own self.

He went to the office three or four times a week usually, and always complained about how hot it was, how much traffic there had been. Rumina didn't know why he even bothered going. She was pretty sure he did absolutely nothing there either.

She had gone with him once. He got to his office, sat in his chair and the office boy had brought tea. Anjum talked on the phone a great deal mostly to his friends, reliving the best moments of the night before and stitching up plans for later. Then, he signed a few papers and that was pretty much that.

'Are you sure you don't have more to do, Anjum?'

'Nope!' Anjum said cheerily, 'Let's go shopping babe!'

'Anjum your father really wants you to go to New York and head up his brother's office there. He's been saying it for years. Why don't we go?' Rumina had said to him over tea as they sat in the garden the evening after Casino night. Anjum had his sunglasses on and was quite sullen. He had only just woken up and it was 5.

'Please babe. Can we not talk about my father?'

'We aren't talking about your father Anjum. We are talking about you and me,' she became emboldened as restlessness turned to desperation.

'We've talked about this before,' she added encouragingly.

'You said it was a possibility, and you would get my status sorted out first. Have you done that?' Anjum said nothing sipping his tea while he smoked.

'Anjum? Talk to me...'

'Why you want to leave Pakistan babe?'

'What do you mean? Why not? Look around you.'

'Yeah exactly. Look around you.'You think we could live like this abroad? No way! Servants? Cars? This house? No wayyyy babe no wayyy!' Anjum said shaking his head, 'Actually, I really hate it abroad.'

'What?'

Rumina recalls how astounded she had been at his revelation. Anjum had explained that he hated travelling on the subways and trains in America and England. He hated living in a flat, even though it was palatial. He hated not having their own pool as they did in their house in Karachi.

Rumina starts laughing softly to herself as she recalls his explanations. The pool? The fucking pool? Anjum never went near the pool, preferring to swim at Sindh Club. In all the years of their marriage he had not even let her swim because 'of the servants.' There was this gorgeous swimming pool that was tended to every single day that she looked at out of her window — its sparkling blue waters calling her, but no-one ever, ever used it. Water shortage? What water shortage?

She realized sinkingly that evening on the verandah that Anjum did not relish the independence that living in the West brought. He was too softened by the lavish excesses of his pampered lifestyle. He didn't crave freedom. He was a man, he *was* liberated and licensed in a way she would never, ever be. It was an untenable impasse.

As long as he lived in his mirage, he was fully convinced by his illusion of freedom. He didn't care for music and culture. He didn't care about cleaner air, glistening oceans.

He loved his hut at the beach and he could bare his chest and swim in the ocean all he wanted. For a man, no, there was no curb on freedoms after all. 'I don't want to move to London or New York, Rumi. Trust me neither do you. Don't you have everything you want?' She had wanted to scream at him then: 'No — I don't have everything I want. Actually, I don't have *anything* I want.'

Instead she said, 'So you haven't found out about my citizenship?'

'No babes. There's no point! We would actually have to live there for you to get anything!'

Something had cracked in her that day. She felt something move like a fault line in the earth, releasing a howling demon that had been haunting her all these years.

Tonight, the demon was with her creating a disturbance, on this night now turning to daybreak.

10

Come In, The Water's Fine

The ground beneath her feet doesn't feel very stable. In fact, she could swear it is moving. She looks around to see if she can find Anjum but he is nowhere to be found. 'Excuse me please,' she doesn't even know who she has been talking to, or what she has been talking about but she knows that she needs to get some fresh air.

The turquoise pool outside is lit up, soothing her as she approaches it gingerly certain she will fall in if she doesn't look where she is going.

She makes her way to a deckchair that is the most concealed from the main party. She eases herself down carefully and after some negotiation with her clutch, her fingers, her lighter and cigarettes — manages to light one.

She doesn't want to get sick — that happened for the first time a few months ago — and it had been a few months since. She doesn't want to re-visit those horrible experiences, hanging onto a toilet bowl at three in the morning. She stares at the pool as it glows with its inner light — cool and inviting. Why were these people so... so... she can't think of the word but she feels it a terrible waste of a pool on this clammy night.

'Hey,' a male voice speaks from somewhere and she sits up as quickly as she can muster on the deckchair but instead manages to fall off it unceremoniously.

'Oh shit! I'm so sorry *yaar*,' the voice is nearer. Through her embarrassment and anxiety, she can feel the strength in the hands helping her up. There is a smell of a piney cologne — with just a touch of sandalwood.

She catches sight of his face and senses she may have seen it before but cannot quite place it. 'Nice to meet you 'properly' — Omar,' he says as he moves a step back having helped her stand up.

'Hi Omar, Gudd… oops Rumina,' she says nearly calling herself by her childhood name.

'Good-Rumina? As opposed to 'Bad-Rumina?" he says quizzically.

She is surprised that a giggle escapes her — a sound alien even to her own ears.

'No, no my name is Rumina,' she pauses and uncharacteristically says, 'But you can call me Guddi if you like.' He smiles.

'Ah! I see. Well than I'm a lucky guy.' She feels embarrassed but at ease at the same time.

'Are you okay Guddi?' Rumina or now Guddi, again stares at him unsure what to say. No-one has asked her that in a long time and before she can reply she feels something welling up inside and before she knows it — she is crying.

'Oh my god, I am so sorry. You don't even know me. I'm just a mess,' she manages to say.

'Actually — I do know you. I've seen you many, many times. I talked to you once too, it was a while ago at a party… well I should say a rather raunchy party!' he pauses giving her time to recollect.

He continues when she doesn't reply.

'I also know that you're a friend of Kiran Alam's, and that you're the wife of Anjum Dadabhoy. So…'

'Oh my god...'

'No, please I didn't tell you that to make you less comfortable, but more... I'm not going to tell anybody if that's what you're worried about,' he puts his hand on hers.

'Trust me. I'm no society guy,' as he says that — he winks and affects a mock pout that makes her laugh. He hands her a tissue and as she dries her tears and composes herself, she feels distinctly better — letting it all out had been cathartic.

'I really need to sit down.'

'Sounds like a plan' he says as he sits down on the deckchair next to her.

'Cigarette?'

'Sure.' As she smokes, she starts to place his face. He had been at Raani's party! He was the mysterious guy who had told her he knew what she was thinking.

'So okay,' she says finally turning to him, 'you somehow know so much about me. Who are you?'

'A friend,' he says smiling.

'Why are you a friend? No-one else is,' as she says this she marvels at her own candour.

'Because I know where you're coming from,' he quickly replies.

'Where's that?'

'Not here!'

She laughs again at his riddles, finding them refreshing. She is too drunk to make sense of anything, and for now it is just nice to feel like someone understands her whether he is putting it on or not.

Taking off her strappy high heels and placing them aside, she dangles her feet in the waters of the pool. He comes and sits next to her, 'You don't mind I hope,' he says in a polite voice.

'I just don't think you should sit so close to the pool unaccompanied... in this present... you know... "state".' He uses air-quotes.

'I can swim... don't worry... although right now... hmmm.' She makes a face that indicates how drunk she is and they both crack up.

'You never used to drink...' Omar says quietly almost as if to himself.

'What? What do you mean, "Used to"?'

He looks at her square in the face and she says, 'Well?' demanding an answer.

'Actually I... I used to know you when you were Guddi,' he looks away at the water and wishes he could say the next part, 'I had a massive crush on you, but you didn't know I existed,' but does not have the courage.

As he looks down at his knees, he seems to Guddi like a very young boy, 'My name is Omar Rafique.'

Guddi racks her alcohol-addled brain, Omar Rafique, Omar Rafique and then a light-bulb goes off. Rabia's brother? She looks at him closely again, and finds herself thinking about how handsome he is with his dark eyebrows, brown eyes, and thick black hair. She remembers him from when she had been to Rabia's house, and the few times she had gone with them for ice-cream or *chaat*.

Despite only being a year or so younger — Omar had

seemed like such a boy and yet this was a man sitting in front of her. 'Omar?' She asks tentatively, 'Like braces and Batman Omar?'

'Yes miss,' he says, now it was his turn to be embarrassed.

'Oh my god! You're Rabia's brother! This is nuts!'

He just smiles and looks even more embarrassed.

'Why haven't you come up to me sooner?'

'Well I was waiting for the right time, I guess.'

'Oh, like when I was completely drunk?'

'Don't be silly I didn't know you were drunk and for your information I didn't follow you out here! I needed to get out of the hello *jaani* hello darrling scene,' he says flailing his hands in mockery.

She laughs at this, 'Yeah these things can be pretty boring! But why are you here anyway? I HAVE to go to these things, but what's your excuse?'

He is quiet for a moment, 'Oh some friends just dragged me here. They often do. They're scared that I don't socialize enough. I spend a lot of time working, and according to them not enough time looking at women!'

'Well that's a new one. Haven't heard of a guy in Karachi who isn't chasing women!'

'Can I be frank?' he asks.

'Sure. At this point, there's no reason not to be.'

'I come to these things 'cos I always kinda hope I'll see you.'

Guddi doesn't know what to say. She is struck by how the thought '*I'm married*' enters her head — almost like a security system. However, she also observes — she does not feel the need to feign outrage or tell him off. She knows that she should just get up and leave as it didn't behoove a rich man's wife to be sitting out here, in this way — but she doesn't want to. She just doesn't want to.

She has never experienced anything even remotely close to this connection and for the first time in her life feels like it is okay to just be. She doesn't know what possesses her next, but she leans forward to kiss him. As her lips touch the warm skin of his, she feels something. She actually feels *something*.

This was new — feeling things. Like the kick of the first spoonful of mixed spicy-sweet *chaat*, the first crack of thunder in a storm. The kiss lasts for a millionth of a second and then Omar pulls away. He holds her with both his hands on her bare arms, and looks at her intently. 'Guddi,' he says, 'This can't be happening.'

They sit in silence, and after a while he says: 'I know you're not happy,' she doesn't even bother to protest or question him and merely says with a half- laugh.

'How can you tell?'

'Your eyes.'

She smiles worriedly at this strange wealth of knowledge about her that Omar seems to possess.

'What are you going to do?' he asks.

'About what?' she says moving her feet in slow circles in the water.

'About being happy?'

She looks at him — startled, and stares off into the pool. She notices the glowing waters of the pool are moving silently with the warm breeze as if, she thinks to herself — invisible people were swimming in it.

She can smell the jasmine and her beloved *motia* overpowering her senses. In the distance, the murmur of voices mixes in with music. She finally replies blankly, 'I hadn't really thought about doing anything.'

'Well Guddi,' he says looking straight at her, 'How about you start... thinking?'

She gives him a look that he cannot decipher and then a split-second later jumps into the pool fully clothed and swims to the other end. When she gets there, she takes a huge lungful of breath and leans against the side of the pool grinning. He is standing there rather gobsmacked.

'How's that for a start?' she says.

'Not quite what I had in mind... but actually not bad... not bad at all ...' and jumps in.

III
Epilogue

The Door

There is that moment between waking and sleeping when you feel fully aware of everything and yet are dreaming. The *hypnagogic* state. She is in a vast sand desert — desolate and bewilderingly beautiful at the same time. Her feet are not touching the ground. She glides along searching feverishly for something — swooping around large tangle weeds — changing direction for no reason at all.

The desert is shimmering in a heat sheen. She realizes she is naked. That alarms her. But there is nothing she can do. She sees a black shape very far away and no matter how fast she propels herself — she cannot reach it. The shape constantly changes form. It is long and human-like, then it becomes round and blob-like.

A large lizard, completely white, scuttles by. She is terrified of lizards and so becomes motionless, hoping it won't notice her. It moves on. She looks back at the horizon and there is no black shape anymore, only a massive white rock cliff.

On top of the cliff is some kind of structure with a door. The door is glowing. She knows she has to reach it. As she feels she is getting nearer, she can hear a throbbing — as if the door is emitting the sound.

She does not know how to reach the door, but once she reaches the foot of the cliff — she starts floating lightly upwards. The deep pulsing sound gets louder and louder. She realizes she is holding a kite in one hand. It is a magnificent viridian, gold and blood-coloured structure — each corner of it flapping like wings. She can go anywhere she wants with this kite. She can go to the door if she chooses or fly higher.

But she wants to open the door. She has to know what is behind the door. She is standing outside it now, and the kite has left her hand. She finds she glides through the door as if it were made of air.

On the other side of it is a mirror in which she can see a heart beating. She believes it is her own, and gasps clutching her chest with fear.

Her grandmother appears an apparition in white. '*What colour is the heart Rumina? What colour is the heart?*' She notices with alarm the heart is turning black before her very eyes.

* * * * * *

Rumina wakes up in a cold sweat. She looks around her room, and discerns it is morning. She is alone. She gets out of bed and walks over to the mirror. Her eyes are red-rimmed. *My skin looks blotchy* she thinks. *My hair is a mess.* She hasn't had it straightened in ages. She doesn't want to.

It wasn't *her* heart in the dream, no, she is sure of it. It was his. His whoring bastard heart. She had tried to throw herself back into her marriage. She had felt so guilty about kissing another man.

I tried like a fool she tells her reflection.

Turns out she needn't have bothered. He had never stopped his old ways. He had been sleeping with whoever he wanted, whenever he wanted since the first week they had been married.

'*Thank God for Kiran. My ally on the inside. And yet I have been waiting. For what I don't know. For a star to fall?*'

Rumina crouches down to reach under her bed, pulls

out a few Louis Vuitton suitcases and begins to pack — slow at first and then in a frenzy; pulling things out of drawers, cupboards and shoving them into the suitcases.

She throws on her long silk kimono over her flimsy nightdress. She picks up her sunglasses and lodges them carefully on her face. She picks up the intercom on the bedside, and asks the driver to be ready with the car. The guard at the gate tells her that the driver is saying his prayers, and will be done in five minutes.

She puts the receiver back in its cradle... her arm swings up in a strong, quick movement across the face of the wall, forcing all but one framed image to fall, glass panels shattering upon reaching the ground.

Rumina picks up her suitcases, and walks out. She has *never* felt this clear in her life.

On the wall, a single photograph of Guddi and Ami Jaan swings on one nail. Ami Jaan's eyes sparkle.

Paani: Water

* 1 *

This was the big one, and Akram knew it. All his life he had worked in or near his village in various capacities for the feudal families that employed him. No matter how wealthy — there was always an element of familiarity.

The families knew exactly who he was, where he lived, the family *he* belonged to — his uncle would have worked as their driver, his grandfather might have been the bearer for their grandfathers or perhaps their cook had married his sister. He had always moved around working for different branches within the same family tree and this suited him well.

Akram was loyal and devoted to his employers and to his family. He had been supporting his ailing mother, father and siblings, since his father lost his sight.

This particular venture, however, would take him away from them — far, far away — to Karachi. He had not ventured more than 129.8 kilometres from home — the distance to Lahore on tasks for his employer — at 1,311.4 kilometres, Karachi was another country.

He had known immediately that he was going to go. His employer's brother had needed a man and had taken a shine to Akram and as much as Mr. Ghulam Ali was loathe to let him go, he had dutifully informed him of the opportunity.

It was more money for one. He could become a rich man, perhaps even be the first in his family to buy a car. Such thoughts kept him company on the bone-rattling two day train ride from Sialkot to Karachi. By the time he arrived, he was surprised he even remembered his name — the bones of his skull seemed to have slid out of their normal positions and his thoughts were shaken.

Karachi City Station — McLeod Station in Colonial times, was a seething, organic mass of people on foot crossing the same unpaved paths as vehicles attempting to get in and out despite the high water on the ground.

He had heard about the monsoons of Karachi. As he traversed the squelching dirt roads of the station, leading to the rickshaw and taxi stands that had turned to mud — he realized he had better lift his *shalwar* slightly. He didn't want to show up at his new employer's house unkempt and dirty.

Mr. Ghulam Ali's brother had sent the driver to receive Akram. In one hand, he clutched his tatty maroon leather valise that his father had pulled out from under his *charpai* on the eve of his departure. He told him that it had been in the family for generations which was hard to doubt by the look of it. It was as if it had literally been dragged through time and space through the generations — Akram had thought, but accepted the heirloom graciously.

As he held the two legs of his loose *shalwar* bunched up in one hand, and his case in the other — he kept a look-out for a big white Pajero as he had been told. He noticed the light of Karachi was different from home — warm and yellow, and the air seemed surprisingly fresh.

This he would soon learn was because of the rain. Surveying the surge of humanity, donkey carts, dare-devil rickshaws and small Suzuki vans — he felt eager to see the rest of the city that would be his new home. Akram was excited.

A man in a white uniform was gesticulating and yelling out to him.

'Hey you — Are you Akram?' Akram saw the stately,

white Pajero standing next to the man calling out to him and hurried across the lot as best as he could without getting splashes of mud all over him.

'*Assalam-A Laikum*!' Akram greeted the driver effusively.

'*Wa Laikum*,' the driver replied, '*Theek thaak*? All well?'

'*Ji ji bilkuul*. Yes, yes, absolutely!' Throwing his valise in the back seat, Akram clambered into the front seat of the car, that the elderly driver had opened for him before walking himself round to the driver's seat.

'*Mera naam Laal Chacha*. My name is Red Uncle,' said the driver, before he started up the engine. Akram noticed Laal Chaca's hair and beard were dyed fluorescent, burnished orange with henna and his teeth were stained through, a darker red — with betel juice, both things that gave him comfort. It was a trope he was familiar with — there were many 'Red Uncles,' where he came from and indeed, in the country. All named for their propensity to dye their hair and beards with henna.

He had been anxious about meeting the Karachi servants. He was told by his colleagues back home that some may be stuck-up — Laal Chaca though was just the sort of person he had needed to greet him.

'*Chacha ji aap se mill ke buhat khushi hoee. Me Akram*! My dear Red Uncle — it is a pleasure to meet you. I am Akram,' he said as the large vehicle started up with the kind of sound only a vehicle with the power of 190 horses and 325 pound-feet of torque could.

2

Akram roamed the confines of the massive bungalow, that was to be his new home for the first few weeks in awe and trepidation — he was afraid he might bump into an expensive looking ornament and smash it irreparably.

He had never seen a house so palatial. The old style landlords *havelis* he was accustomed to were based in the old Mughal style — a courtyard in the centre, wooden pillars and large sprawling rooms with lots of air and ventilation. Plants, flowers and trees would be laid out everywhere in the courtyard.

This architecture was different. Vertical glistening marble — so dazzling in the sun with its tall, narrow, rectangular windows — tinted with coated black-out material to shield against the cruel Karachi heat. The marble floors inside ensured the interior too remained cool. Giant columns held terraces and balconies up whilst pillars adorned the entranceway. There was something unsettling to Akram, about the almost antiseptic cold of the house — walls and floors should never be able to hold your reflection that way, he thought.

'*Haan Akram baboo... Karachi logon ka essh-tyle hee faraq hain, nai?* So Akram what do you think? Karachi people have a certain finesse, is it not?' Laal Chacha had said chewing and spitting his evening *paan* after a hard day's work driving various members of his employer's family around the fecund, organic, restless rill of Karachi roads.

The new employers, Mr. and Mrs. Rehmat Ali — had been very welcoming of Akram, as had their entire staff of servants; gardeners, drivers, *chowkidars*, young maids, elderly maids or *ammas*, cooks — bearers. Akram could hardly figure out why they had needed him at all.

Mr. Rehmat Ali — however, was clear on the fact that he needed a trustworthy, sensible manservant that he could be sure would not steal from him, and would be able to run errands for him alone — as well as manage all the other servants. It was with these express requirements of his brother's in mind, that Ghulam Ali had offered Akram to his brother.

Ghulam Ali's children were now married off, and he and his wife were planning to spend time travelling around the country and the globe visiting all of them. He figured taking the position at his brother's, would be better for Akram than tending to an empty house.

Mr. Rehmat Ali was a great fan of *shikaar*, or hunting for sport and Akram learnt he was to accompany him on these hunting trips and would tend to his guns. Akram had never been on *shikaar* before and found the prospect quite thrilling. Upon arrival, Mr. Rehmat Ali began teaching him all that he needed him to know about the rifles and shotguns, and the cleaning of them — in order to prepare Akram before taking him on a trip.

Akram became accustomed to the daily rituals quickly — he had many years of experience. Wake up, oversee the cooks and maids setting out breakfast for the family. If Mr. Rehmat Ali was taking his tea and toast in the study and not in the dining room than he, Akram was to take it to him with the newspapers, and check if he had anything for him to do.

After the members of the household went off to schools, office — coffee mornings, as Mrs. Rehmat Ali was wont to do, Akram oversaw the cleaning of the vast mansion. He also made sure the gardeners did not sit around smoking *biddhis*, although if he was perfectly honest since the house and garden were tended every single day — some days they could afford to have a few more tea and *biddhi* breaks. He made sure that lunch preparations were started well in time, that *Amma*, the senior-most maid was attending to the laundry and that the junior driver was taking the clothes to the dry cleaner.

There was no end — Akram realized to the needs of these rich Karachi families and he loved the work. He relished manning this army of servants and he reveled in the pace of life here. Things were so slow in Sialkot. Akram felt his capabilities had never been utilized to their fullest potential till now.

As the days turned into weeks, Akram found himself surer and surer that he had made the right choice. He talked to his family a few times on the telephone and they seemed to be doing fine.

He had sent so much money back, from his first month advance, that they were overjoyed and the eldest of his younger brothers had now stepped in to take care of the family in his stead. He went to sleep every night after saying his *namaaz* and thanking Allah for all his blessings.

3

Every four or five days, a white van pulled up at the house between 12 p.m. and 2 p.m. Three men in blue shirts and trousers with name badges would wheel in a retinue of heavy, thick plastic barrels full of 'purified' water. They would make three trips, each one of them wheeling in three at a time.

Akram would escort them to the storage room where these containers were to be kept. He would take the receipt, after which they would proceed to wheel the collection of empty water barrels in there, back out to the van.

He would then show them out. Following which, for about an hour or more, it was his job to organize the distribution of the barrels. The odd-job boys, Chota 1 (Small One #1) and Chota 2 (Small One #2) were his helpers in the enterprise.

'Go upstairs and bring any remaining empty barrels down,' Akram would order the little helpers. This was not the easiest of jobs for them. It involved going to every single room in the house; the master bedroom, the master bathroom, Choti Bibi and Baby's bathrooms, Chotey Saab's bathroom, Dadi Bibi's room, collect all the unwieldly barrels and bring each one, one at a time — down the stairs.

It was when they started carrying the full barrels up that the complaining would reach fever pitch. They would grumble and overact, '*Itna barra ghar to Lift to daal detay.*' — 'Such a grand house. They could have installed a lift!' Chota 1 (tutting with his tongue on his teeth). '*Buhat paisay. Kum aql.* Lots of money, no common sense.' Chota 2.

Akram did think a lift would be a good idea, after

all carrying the barrels full of water upstairs one at a time was no easy job. They weighed 19kg each, and it was almost impossible for Chota 1 and Chota 2 to load them onto the water dispensers. That was Akram's job, once they were all in place. Initially, he had had a few disasters himself whilst trying to do this. A few times the barrel had slipped spilling water everywhere, than he had slipped on the water and fallen on his behind.

How Chota 1 and Chota 2 had laughed. He had yelled at them and chased them off to get cleaning materials, 'Go get the *taaki* rag and get back here and clean this mess up!' he ordered them imperiously.

He was mystified by these barrels from the start. When he first saw them dotted all over the house — he had laughed, as it was strange to see such things in a house. Usually he had seen them in offices.

Perhaps, he thought Mr. Ali owns a company that provides these services, or manufactures these bottles. But did they really need so many? As he became more intimate with the private quarters of the family he was further mystified. Why did they need one in every bathroom AND bedroom as well as five just in the kitchen, and one in every room downstairs. How much water did these people really need to drink?

And really — why did they need it bottled and provided this way? Was there not water in the taps? Was there a serious water problem in the house, in the area, in the city of Karachi? He had heard of water problems in the city and severe load-shedding. He knew Karachi had the worst electrical supply in the whole country.

As he soaped himself with the bubblegum pink LifeBuoy soap in the servant quarter bathroom every morning, expecting the water to whittle down to a trickle, or for there to be nothing when he turned it on — he realized there was no such problem here.

In fact, he had never experienced such a steady supply of hot water in his whole life. He also discovered that a water tanker actually visited the house, and all the houses in the neighbourhood on a weekly basis. So why the white van as well? One thing was certain he wrote in a letter to his younger brother:

'There is no shortage of water in this house.'

* 4 *

The cooks were preparing dinner for the family. A large metal pot was on the stove with chopped onions, garlic, turmeric, cumin, and red chilli powder sizzling in the oil. The redolence of a feast to come created a haze in the kitchen. Spirited cooks were chopping meats and preparing seasonings.

Akram had noticed a few strange things in the kitchen as well.

Twice a week when fruits and vegetables were bought fresh from the market, huge tubs were filled with water from the dispensers. Baboo Ji, the gray-haired senior cook of thirteen years would then go around to each tub and add granules that would enter the water painting it a deep beetroot pink.

Sometimes he would add a white tablet as well — or instead, that fizzed up and dissolved upon contact. Then the fruits and vegetables were left to soak for about 40 minutes. Akram made the mistake once of taking the apples out before the prescribed 40 minutes and than proceeded to wash them under the tap in the sink assuming that this pink stuff had to be rinsed off.

There was hell to pay with Baboo Ji that afternoon. He told Akram to lay off and leave this work to him, and never do that to any fruit that the Alis would be consuming. Akram was convinced that the pink stuff would poison him but Baboo Ji assured him it was not poisonous, it was just to make sure everything was 'extra clean'. Akram had sniffed an apple before biting into it, but to his surprise he had found there was no bitter or acrid taste in his mouth that should not be there; it was all apple.

The other thing was that — whenever a recipe called for water, it was added from the bottled water and not from the tap. When tea was made it was also the bottled water. He realized that this was why there were five water receptacles just in the kitchen alone.

However, he and the others drank from a clay *matka* in the corner of the kitchen using the tin cups that sat there by it, and he was pretty certain that it was filled from the tap. One day he decided to try the Special Water and discover for himself its magical properties. He walked over with a glass and poured himself the water.

'What are you doing Akram?' Baboo Ji asked

'I'm drinking water of course.'

'No, no, no, no, no! That is for Saab and Begum Saab and the family only! We don't drink that water. That is *their* water,' said the cook indicating with his eyes the Master and Mistress of the house upstairs. Akram was perplexed.

'Well anyway I've poured this so I'll drink it!' As he took the gulp, he expected sparks to shoot from his eyes, wings to sprout from his feet, or perhaps, he would settle for a tingling feeling in his bones. 'It's... nice and sweet?' he ventured, uncertain if the water was in fact any different from any other water but clearly had to comment after staging his rebellion.

'You even cook with it!' Akram said to Baboo Ji who was busy stirring the contents of his family-size stainless steel saucepan.

'Well they have asked us to,' He was busy with his cooking and giving orders to the second-in-command. Just then Booa the eldest maid came in and Baboo Ji said to her, 'Akram here is getting all excited about the water!' She laughed and said, 'What's to get excited about?'

'They have it in the bathrooms too Booa. Do they even bathe with it? Clean their bums with it? What's wrong with the water in the taps? And if there's something wrong with it, why do *we* drink it?' Booa laughed even harder.

'You are a curious fellow. They like it. That's all. They're rich! They can do what they like. Now you better go into the dining room and make sure those stupid girls set the table right. Go on!'

Akram went to attend to his duties, and decided to wait and see if perhaps the effects of the water would creep up on him later.

✳ 5 ✳

'Akram! Akram!'

'Yes Madam?' Akram rushed to where the lady of the house was calling from.

'Akram, I have to rush off. I needed to let you know that the company that was delivering the water will no longer be coming. There will be a different company, and they're going to come today. The old company will come by to get the rest of their empty barrels but that will be later in the week.'

'Ok?'

The new people will bring the same amount and your work will be the same but I just wanted you to know so you're not surprised. Here's the money to tip them,' she handed him 500 ruppees as she always did for all three delivery men, and was gone. Akram's curiousity was piqued.

When they arrived there was nothing too different about them. Instead of a white van they had a blue van, and the delivery men were in similar uniforms. It was all pretty much the same routine and the water looked the same. The only thing that was different were the stickers on the canisters. They were gold in colour and shaped like crowns.

Clearly, Akram surmised, this must be the King, the *Badshah* of Waters... When he saw the numbers penned on the receipt that the delivery men handed him he was certain that this was the King of Waters. It cost more than he made in half a year, and there were about ten of these deliveries in a month. Shaking his head, he went back inside to make sure all the barrels were in order and the boys hadn't made a mess of things.

Akram grew to like Mr and Mrs Rehmat Ali and their children immensely. They were polite and caring and never treated him with disrespect. He was grateful to Allah for making his situation so pleasant despite what he had heard about these Big City Folk.

Most of all he loved Choti Bibi — Little Miss — the Rehmat Ali's youngest daughter. She was the apple of her parent's eye and kept everyone in the house laughing with her effusive personality and antics. After school, she would sit with the servants in the kitchen and chat with them whilst eating a snack of samosas and tea or kebabs — sharing with them stories of school.

Akram grew very protective of Choti Bibi and felt it his duty to give her advice on various matters, such as how to handle bullying boys, conniving girls and punishing teachers.

'Choti Bibi you must work hard in school. Your parents are so proud of you. You must make sure you get good marks and become a very famous lady!'

'Yes, yes,' Baboo Ji would agree, 'Listen to Akram. He's a sensible fellow'.

'Yeah but why should I work hard in Maths? I haaaatttee maths! What good is maths to me?' she would say.

'Bibi you are very lucky to be going to school with good teachers and without Maths you won't know anything at all! Maths is very important. Right Baboo Ji?'

'Yes, yes Maaats, Maaats!' Baboo Ji repeated absent-mindedly, engrossed in separating and putting away his vast treasure of brightly coloured, aromatic spices.

'Anyway,' said Choti Bibi giggling at the cooks pronunciation of 'maths', 'the teacher said she would send me to the principal if I did not start paying attention!'

Akram looked concerned. Choti Bibi laughed, 'Please Akram don't look so worried! I won't go to the principal's office. I will be a good girl instead! Happy?... I definitely WON'T pass notes to my friends in class,' she added and with that flounced out of the kitchen.

They could hear her footsteps as she ran clattering in sandals up the shiny white marble stairs to her bedroom.

* * * * *

Akram was working with the gardeners making sure they planted the right seeds. Choti Bibi came into the garden to see what was happening.

'Oof more gardening!'

Akram smiled, 'But it's nice Bibi. Look how beautiful your garden is!'

'I know. I know. But Mummy just never stops!' she said skipping off.

'You know Akram the summer holidays will start soon and guess what! We're going to London for three weeks! All of us!'

'Very good Bibi. Very good,' he nodded happily.

Akram hadn't been told as yet of Mr. and Mrs. Rehmat Ali's plans, but was sure the servants would be pleased to also have some time off from their duties.

The blue water van drove through the gate. They had missed a day and so had to re-schedule for that weekend.

Choti Bibi followed Akram watching the proceedings, and even offering to help which Akram immediately vetoed.

'No Bibi there is no way I would let you do that!' She watched as he loaded the lofty barrels onto the dispensers.

'God I am so sick of Mummy and Daddy's rules about water! Do you know Akram that we are not even allowed to brush our teeth with tap water!'

Akram was very interested to get some insight into the water rituals of the family. 'So that's why you have them in the bathrooms!'

'Of course!' said Choti Bibi, 'and you know sometimes by mistake I have just turned on the tap and started brushing my teeth without thinking and then I get so scared that I'm going to get sick, and maybe even DIE!!'

Akram laughed at this, 'Bibi I drink water from the tap and brush my teeth. I'm fine! Why would you die?'

'No Akram, I could die. There are diseases in the water in Pakistan you know!' 'Really?' said Akram, 'YEAH!' Choti Bibi replied already bored with the subject and ran off.

Akram thought about what he had learnt as he performed his duties for the day. What did she mean by she could die? What diseases were these that were in the water? In Sialkot, he knew of some people nearer to the city who boiled the water in great big cooking pots in their homes, but he was not aware of germs so dangerous in the water that they could kill you.

If that was the case, why was he and everyone he knew not dead? He watched day in and day out as the Ali's consumed copious amounts of bottled water, paying amounts on which a family could subsist for a whole year with everything included; rent, food, clothing, petrol for a motorbike, school — and even outings once a week.

On his visits to Mr. Ali's offices he saw the same water receptacles positioned everywhere. The building was a massive one with more levels than Akram could count but on the floor that he visited alone there were hundreds.

He was anxious through the night imagining the illnesses that were going to assail him because he had not been aware of the deadly germs that had been lurking in the water — all the unwashed fruit and vegetables he had ever eaten, all the water he had drunk was going to come and get him.

From never giving these matters a second thought — he now felt a sense of unease, not present before.

The summer holidays rolled around and before he knew it the family had packed up and gone off to London.

'Don't worry about much in our absence,' Mr. Ali had said, 'Think of it as a paid vacation!'

There was still a small army of servants to feed but the pressure was naturally much reduced, and many of them also took the opportunity to visit their families.

During the break, every evening — all the servants who remained at the house, gathered in the living room to sit on the floor and watch television till the early hours of the morning. None of them was ready to break all protocol and sit on the furniture — in case it somehow got back to the Rehmat Alis.

They drank endless cups of tea and a few of them would regularly go outside to smoke the pungent *bidis*. Some nights they would sit outside with Nisar the watchman smoking hookahs and gazing at the stars.

'This is the life,' Akram thought pleased with himself for having made the move from Sialkot to Karachi — the anxiety he had felt a far-off memory. The three weeks came to an end before they knew it and despite the fun they were having — they were glad and slightly relieved to get back to being busy, when the family returned.

The servants lined up outside to welcome them — in clean clothes, polished shoes and tamed hair. A far cry from the dishevelled and unkempt look most of them had been sporting for the three weeks past.

'Welcome back Saab!' Akram greeted Mr. Ali — enthusiastically rushing off to help Laal Chacha and the younger driver with the luggage, as both the cars had gone to pick them up. The children rushed about excited to be home. Akram had tea and biscuits served in the garden room.

'So — Akram,' said Mrs. Ali, 'Everything alright in our absence?'

'Yes Bibi. No problem,' he said in uncertain English.

'That's very good, and the house looks spic and span — so thank you.'

Akram retreated and let them unwind and chat. Choti Bibi came running out a little while later and found him in the kitchen.

'Akrrraaammmm!'

'*Asalamalaikum* Choti Bibi!'

'Oh my god! Akram — London was soooo big and soooo many lights and soooo many black taxis and did you know they have these huge buses that are double-decker like a sandwich!'

'Really?' he could not imagine what she meant. She rushed off to find something and came back waving a piece of cardboard in his face. 'See, See!' Akram looked closely at what was a postcard. There was indeed a photograph of what looked like glowing, jolly, red, tall buses on it.

'You're right Bibi,' he said, 'They are like a double-decker sandwich!' he was just as amazed as his young ward at the wonder of these London buses.

'Akram you know what else? In London you can turn on the taps and drink and drink and drink water like this..' She made a greedy, gobbling gesture with her hands towards her mouth and Akram laughed and laughed, '*Haan*! Yes! Any tap in the bathroom even! I wasn't used to it so at first I asked my mother how I should brush my teeth, and she said it's okay *beta* just use the taps!'

'*Wah*!' said Akram. Booa who had been listening to the last part of the conversation said, '*Haan* but you're back now and you better not forget that you have to use the barrel and not the taps!'

'Yes, yes,' said the little girl.

'It was so nice to just be NORMAL like people on TV! When I grow up I'm going to live in London and drink water from my taps day in and day out!' she pronounced scuttling off just as she had scuttled in.

'Booa does everyone in the city drink this water?' Akram asked his colleague gesturing towards the water dispenser.

'Yes, I think so. My sister works in a house in Defence and a cousin in another house and they say everyone does that. Apparently they believe the water is not safe.'

'In Karachi...' he mumbled contemplatively.

'Not in Karachi brother. Our country's water, Pakistani water, is contaminated!'

'But how come I have never heard this before?'

'We are poor folk Akram. We are not as important. Why should anyone care if we drink dirty water or not? So why should they educate us? Besides what will we do? We can't afford this water they drink. You would think it was made of gold!' she laughed a toothless, *paan*-stained laugh.

'Anyway. You and I are alive no? It can't be that bad. These rich people get scared easily!'

'Yes, I suppose you're right,' conceded Akram.

7

Over time, Akram learnt that the Ali's paranoia went much deeper than he had imagined. None of them were allowed to drink fresh fruit juice outside of the house, 'Because of *milawat*, or contamination,' Mrs. Ali said as she briefed Akram before he was to act as chaperone for the children. They were to be escorted to the market with the driver for an evening drive to get some snacks.

'Don't let them trick you into having *chaat* either.'

'What's wrong with *chaat* Bibi?' Akram was genuinely surprised that the delicious spicy snack of chickpeas and yoghurt, that everyone in the country ate of an evening snack — was also forbidden.

'Akram they use water in the tamarind sauce, and they wash the onions in the water. So there is no way the children can eat it. There are a few places that now say they use mineral water for everything though, but then we have to be with them to see if it is a legitimate claim or not.'

'Yes Bibi,' Akram could feel his new friend anxiety flickering.

'I know we may seem a little crazy Akram!' Mrs. Ali said as if reading his mind, 'But you cannot be too careful these days. There are so many illnesses that are transmitted through the water. You must have heard of Gastroenteritis? Typhoid? Dysentry?' Akram had heard of these, they were rampant in his village and in the surrounding villages.

'Actually — many children in our extended families and in our village have died from these diseases Bibi,' Akram spoke ever so quietly.

'So has no-one ever taught you about water safety?

The doctors? Don't they tell you at least to boil your water?'

'Boil? No Bibi,' Akram said in a voice that sounded ashamed, 'Akram! I can't believe it!' He just looked down at his feet.

'Have you ever been ill with any of these things?'

'Gaas-Tro-In-Tri-Tris,' Akram said struggling to pronounce the strange word that doctors had hurled at him many-a-time — that meant to him tummy aches, diarrhoea and sometimes vomiting.

'That can get more serious if you don't watch how and what you eat and drink, you know?'

By now Akram didn't know what to think or say so just nodded his head and said, '*Ji Bibi*. Yes Ma'am.'

What was the use? Her questions had convinced him he was going to die. They were all going to die and nobody cared because they were poor and only the rich got to live because they could spend One lac ruppees a month buying *Khuda Kaa Paani*, Water Of Allah Himself, he thought darkly.

As he lay in his room that night he realized he was glad at least he finally knew the mystery of the water — as alarming as the information was. Even though Mrs. Ali had seemed genuinely concerned — he wondered if she was just a mad, overly cautious rich woman as Booa had said.

Nonetheless, he had poured a glass of water from the water dispenser in the kitchen to drink before sleeping. This time he was sure he could feel the difference. It was as if the water was coursing through his veins cleaning out the illnesses and germs — like a wiper on a windshield — as he fell asleep.

8

The next day they were all roused by Mrs. Ali who called them into the lounge.

'Have you not been drinking boiled water as I asked you all to?'

Nobody seemed to know what she was talking about. The truth was that someone had been told to do so but didn't see what all the fuss was about. Booa who was a veteran in the household and so least afraid to speak said, '*Bibi hum to poori zindagi nalkay ya kooay ka pani peetay ai hain. To hume to koi fikr nahi, aap bhi fikr na kejeeay.* Ma'am we've been drinking tap water or well water our whole lives. If we are unconcerned, there is no cause for you to be.'

Akram who was resolutely staring at his feet, looked up to see Mrs. Ali's expression. She was obviously having none of it. Appointments had been made for every single one of them at the private hospital which a close friend of Mr. Ali's owned — and they were all to have blood tests, and physical examinations. In addition, the doctor would explain to them at length about the effects of drinking unsanitary water. They all went to their rooms to get ready to leave.

Choti Bibi came running down, she still had a few days of summer vacation left, 'Akram Akram Where are you all going?' Akram explained to her and Choti Bibi said 'See! I told you! Mummy is very VERY careful because I had another brother and he died from the water from TIEFOYD!' Akram was shocked.

'Choti Bibi?'

'Ya-ah it's true. Ask my Mummy! You better go get ready,' she said as she dashed off again.

Akram took the steps to his room at a slow, measured pace — as things became clearer. He could lose someone just as they had.

That night after the eventful and informative day Akram wrote a letter home:

Dearest Ami Jaan, Mother Darling,

Life in the big city is going well. My employers continue to treat me very well, and I am very happy. I hope you are enjoying getting so much more money every month. I am writing to you to share with you some new things I have learnt. The Begum Saab here is a very caring woman and she has told me that I need to be more careful with water.

The water in our Beloved Pakistan Ami I am sorry to tell you is poisoning us. You know all those children that have died in the village? It was because they drank dirty water. I know you may not believe me. I didn't believe it either, but it is true.

The doctor talked to all of us servants for a long time and explained it all to us. Ami, I want you to do one thing for me. Ask your daughters-in-law to do it.

They MUST from now on BOIL all the water for at least an hour. Go and buy big pans and before you fill the matkas — boil all the water. I will check on all of you and make sure you are doing this.

You must promise to do this for me. I want to see my family live a long and healthy life.

With Much Love and Respect to you and Father, Your Son, Akram.

9

When the blood tests came back every single member of the domestic staff had some form of a water-borne stomach illness from mild gastroenteritis to amoebic dysentry. Akram was shocked at the results.

He had not escaped either and had discovered he had a mild infection in his stomach lining as well. Antibiotics were prescribed, a stricter watch on where and what they ate and drank to be kept. Mr and Mrs Ali footed all the bills.

Many of them grumbled at the rigours, some insisted that they had been fine so far, so what if they had some bad bacteria in their bellies? The junior cook said he was sure everyone who lived in Karachi had them. The Alis realized that it would be too expensive if everyone used the bottled water, so the boiled water was a must for the staff and any other measures were obviously recommended but at their own discretion.

Akram followed everything the doctor and Mrs. Ali had told him to a tee. He personally took charge of the boiling of the water. It had to continue to simmer for at least 40 minutes after it came to a boil; the cooks would get annoyed with him — wanting to use the burners on the stove but Akram was resolute.

'It's done *murra*!' the junior cook who was a gruff Pathan or Northener would insist, 'it took long enough for such a huge dish of water to start boiling as it is and now... *Boil ho raha hain*! It's boiling. C'mon man that should be fine!'

'It has to sit for another hour Yasir. And that's that,' Akram would say quietly, and Yasir would go off in a huff.

'It's already been over an hour!' But Akram didn't

care. None of the other servants even considered their teeth-brushing habits, but Akram started using boiled water only.

Laal Chacha would howl with laughter as Akram walked up to the bathroom with his jug of water.

'What's happened to you? These rich city people have gotten to you!'

'Laal Chacha doesn't it bother you that all of us came back with some kind of illness or the other?'

'So what! We are strong. Stomachs like cast iron!' he said thumping on his tummy proudly.

'We're used to all the dirt and contamination. If we start changing our habits now who knows!' Laal Chacha was the only one who had refused to change his habits. He had taken the antibiotics because they were free, but beyond that he drew the line.

In time, Akram found that the almost constant semi-off stomach that he had had all his life and more so since he moved to Karachi was getting better. He was very careful with street food as well. He felt silly insisting on *chaat* that had been made using mineral water, as they would probably take one look at him and laugh — so he just stopped eating it. His favourite treat was pomegranate juice freshly squeezed at the juice-wallah from the giant silver metal wheel juicer.

He could only get this once a month as it was quite expensive, and now he watched them closely while they used the large hand-operated silver wheel to extract the juice from the ruby kernels. He did catch a few different juice stalls adding the tap water, so he was even more wary now.

He lost some weight as he had stopped eating treats from the street vendors. Yes, Akram felt — as he would sit in the evenings with Laal Chacha and the other male domestic staff under the stars — he was a new man now, in this city, and he was pleased with himself. His family told him that they were doing as he had told them too. Yes he would think whilst smoking a contemplative *biddi* — he was becoming a man of the world — more aware of things.

After a year of service Akram decided it was time to visit his family at home. The Alis had told him he could go anytime he wanted but Akram had preferred to wait till a year was up. As he stood at the platform waiting for the train he recalled the last time he had been there, was when he had arrived in his new life, in a new city.

On the ride back as he went through lush green landscapes. It occurred to him he hadn't actually seen much green since he had left. His home too, seemed more lush than he remembered.

The air was a shade of fresh he had not experienced in a while. He walked around the fields with his brothers and old friends. Everyone had a question for him — about the big city and the people who lived there and his employers. The local merchants congregated every night at the local *naan* bread shop. They were all very impressed with his status and told him that there had been whisperings that he had become a big man now whose family only drank boiled water.

Akram enjoyed resting and not having to do much but an active man by nature he started missing his work. The morning before he was to leave his brothers took him out to have the traditional Pakistani breakfast of *halwa puri* and *nihari* or meat stew. By the time they were done they were incapable of doing much more than lounge around on the *charpais* that were laid outside in the shade, so heavy was this breakfast. They baked in the sun, napping before heading home.

That night Akram began to get a stomach ache. He had not had one like this in his entire life. He started getting feverish and after a while of tossing and turning he found he had to rush to the bathroom and to his horror could not control either his bowels nor his stomach.

He was in there for hours alternately vomiting and sitting on the toilet. His mother heard the retching noises and came to see if he was alright.

'Akram *beta*. Akram son?'

'*Amma* I am very sick!' he managed to say.

'Hospital *chalo*!' his mother said immediately,

'No, no *Amma*. Let's just see,' he obviously had food poisoning which he'd had often enough when he was younger. But never this bad.

When the vomiting subsided he lay in bed his head spinning and tried to go to sleep. His mother brought in various concocotions smelling of fennel, cumin, turmeric and cinnamon. She sat by his side with a cold compress — his face was burning up. He was sure his brothers would be sick too, but his mother said they were all fine.

'But we all ate the same things!' Akram insisted.

'Nothing? Not even the runs?'

'No,' his mother shook her head.

In his feverish state Akram was perplexed. He was so careful! What could have happened. He replayed the night before. The hot, oily pooris, the steaming, sweet *halw*a, the rich grams in the thick sauce, the thick stew... it made him quite sick thinking of the food again but he continued. He had to get to the bottom of this.

There he was raising a portion to his mouth, than the man brought over water, he didn't drink it. Then he reached over and... the yoghurt. He immediately felt a rising nausea and had to rush to the bathroom. He had eaten the yoghurt. They always mixed water in yoghurt and that was yet another thing that Akram tried to avoid but that evening — he had not paid attention.

His mother got worried about him and called the local doctor requesting him to come over as a favour, as he often did. The doctor took Akram's blood as a safeguard, prescribed some oral rehydration powders, antibiotics and said he would contact them when the results were ready.

Akram could not remember being this ill in all his life, and was angry. He took so much care and had changed his life around and yet he had gotten ill but nobody else. He now had to take more time off and wait till he was better to get back to Karachi.

'Akram I'm sorry to tell you that in addition to food poisoning — you have contracted typhoid,' the doctor told them when he returned to the house, a few days later. Akram felt an icy feeling spread through his chest. He was rendered speechless.

'Will he be alright?' his mother asked.

'He will hopefully be if he takes all the medicines and does exactly what I tell him and you all do too.'

'Of course!'

The doctor launched into a lecture about water — the dangers of water, about the boiling of water and how important it is.

Typhoid fever was highly contagious.

Typhoid is spread through food and water contaminated by human faeces and so forth.

Akram now sure he was delirious, found himself unable to curb his laughter which sounded to him like it was coming from a far off place.

'Why are you laughing?'

Akram listed categorically to the doctor all the things he'd been doing. The doctor heard about the cleaning of the fruit and veg.

He heard about the brushing-teeth-with-boiled-water thing.

'Because doctor I know about these things, I *know*! I don't even eat *chaat* anymore!' Akram seemed to be getting excited 'and doctor I have had my family doing the same. So what do you say to that?'

The grey-haired doctor who was sitting on a chair at Akram's bedside looked at his patient, took off his spectacles and started cleaning them on his *kameez* and made some strange noises like he was suppressing laughter — his shoulders appeared to be shaking.

'Then what can I tell you?' (allowing himself to laugh a little more freely now) 'I've never heard of anyone being *tha*t careful! You must feel like a bit of an idiot now. You might as well have enjoyed your *chaat*. There's shit — human shit in the food from the shit in the water, son! Shit! Dirty shit!'

Akram was nodding in and out of the room. The fan above his bed seemed to be hypnotizing him. It seemed like the doctor was in fact, laughing? He was usually such a serious man too. Akram's predicament seemed to amuse the man, no end.

As the words 'shit in the water' and the doctor's laughter hovered in the air in the realm of his hearing — Akram felt another violent wave of nausea ride through him, as both vomit and excrement shot out of his passages — well into the dawn.

Janat Ki Huwa:
The Air In Paradise

I
Raga Deepak

1

Zainab

It was eight o' clock on a Sunday morning and Javed was already at odds with the day, still in bed after a night disturbed tossing and turning through the variegations of electricity supply. There was no UPS battery, the poor man's generator — in the hostel.

Some nights Javed would stumble into the shared washroom and stand in the shower with his white cotton vest, *shalwar* — and the sheet he slept with wrapped around him, letting the cold water sooth his heat-ravaged body and soul. Then squelching wet he would get back into his bed, soaked — inevitably to be bone-dry within minutes.

He was sitting up with his hands behind his head. The absence of electricity created a void; no fan, no movement, just a weighty, smothering stillness. Through the sole minor window near his bed — the sunlight was filling his room. He stared at his posters of Kareena Kapoor, Raani Mukherji and Ashwariya Rai. Outside the roar of the traffic on the bridge was gearing up. He felt vaguely hungry but had no desire to move.

A loud humming became audible and the blades of the fan on his ceiling had life restored to them. The building was once again abuzz. With the much-coveted breeze caressing his skin — he drifted off to sleep staring at his pin-up ladies and dreaming he was in a large marble palace of pure white — like the Taj.

Kareena was there too, in a turquoise sari — her eyes sparkling like the silver work embroidered on the exquisite thick silk enrobing her. The most palpable quality about the dream was the cool — the sheer and utter cool of the marble palace. He felt light, free. He realized he was wearing a white shirt open at the collar almost down to his belly, and his beloved 'English' trousers.

Later whilst wondering where he got the guts (even if only in dream) — to sport such a look — he decided that after all this was how the Bollywood heroes appeared! When Ajay Devgan was visiting Karachi for a film festival he had his shirt open till his belt buckle — Javed mused, having seen it in a clip on T.V.

In the dream he was Ajay and Kareena was his lady dancing like the sails of a ship coruscating in the wind. But then, his feet started feeling hot. Then his arms felt hot. He looked up at Kareena and she was on fire, and he too was on fire.

There was an unceremonious bang and Javed awoke sitting upright. The blades of the fan were winding down to a menacing stop. The electricity had gone again. The palace melted away like ice-cream. He sat on the edge of his bed running his hands through his hair. He could have sworn his hair felt cooler than it should — as it does when one is in an air-conditioned room.

He looked out of the window with a view of the Cantt train station adorned with garbage piles of all sizes and viscosity and an array of stray dogs, cats and wild birds attacking the piles for food, and realized it was time for him too to have breakfast. A train was pulling out and the sound of it caused the ground beneath his feet to start vibrating — the shrieking ripping through his thoughts. He pulled on some clothes, smoothed his hair, grabbed his keys and headed down to the communal kitchen.

After a meal of a greasy *paratha*, an omlette, and

some tea he headed out towards the sea to his favourite place on a Sunday: *Itwaar* / Sunday Bazaar — the jumble sale of Karachi — oddly hip even with the elite. Many a Sunday, fashion designers, models and an assortment of celebrities major and minor, could be seen scouring the dusty sandy paths for a bargain amongst the used clothing, wrought iron furniture, boxes of old copies of Reader's Digest and bric-a-brac. Everything there was of mysterious provenance. How *did* a tea-cloth commemorating the Queen of England's jubilee get to that market? How did random *Simpson's* memorabilia get there? There were no ready-made businesses for Western ball-gowns, and yet there were ball-gowns.

Javed was fed up of squinting furiously against the astringent sunlight of Karachi. He had bought sunglasses off sellers in the street which provided no protection or relief and invariably broke. He was a man with a plan — moving up and out and so the next step, he had decided was to buy the most impressive specimen of sunglasses his money could buy (and he had been saving up) — so he would at least look the part like the urbane, sophisticates of Karachi.

He figured that sooner or later — if he looked the part, and sounded the part (contingent on his English improving) — he too would eventually be granted the ultimate spoils of what he called the 'English-Medium life' — an air conditioner in his home, air conditioner at his work and an air conditioned car with which to get from home to work and vice versa.

Day into night, week after week — this other imaginary life beckoned to him.

Itwaar Bazaar was proving to be fun that day as there was to be plenty of star-spotting. Javed was sure he had seen that gorgeous girl who played music videos on B4U already, and the terrifying female news anchor with the Egyptian nose and deadened eyes from Sunrise News too was prowling the bazaar. He had seen the hair and make-up guru with almond-shaped, glittering eyes and constantly changing colour of hair who always seemed to Javed to be on T.V., surrounded by glamorous women sporting equally baffling styles of hair.

Javed snuck a few surreptitious photographs with his phone to show to Sher Jaan and the lads at the tea house later. He spotted a rack of chequered shirts and gravitated towards them. At 25 ruppees and dubious origin, he couldn't go wrong. The sweat that had taken up occupation in the three shirts he owned, was getting more and more difficult to wash out.

A boy of no more than 14 — in a taupe *shalwar kameez*, with large rheumy brown eyes and matted hair was manning the stall. 'How much?' Javed asked. '25 Sir,' the young boy replied promptly. Here in *Itwaar* Bazaar amongst the street urchins Javed was 'Sir' and 'Saab,' which caused him to puff up a bit.

'I'll give you 15.'

'No Sir. It's 25,' the young entrepenuer retorted — holding his ground despite being in full cognizance of customary final outcomes of such transactions.

'No boy! Have you gone mad?' Javed gave it some welly and got into the spirit of the rite of passage that was The Haggle.

'What can I do *Saab*?' the boy emoted putting on his most professional miserable face perfected to garner sympathy. But Javed was having none of it — after all he was only a few steps up on the food chain from this lad and he needn't think he had money coming out of his ears just because he was dressed in pant-shirt.

'Okay forget it!' Javed made a pretence of storming off in a huff. Like clockwork, the minute he turned his back and had taken half a step he heard the boy's voice concede: 'Ok Sir, 18,' Javed gave the child 20 ruppees picked up the red, mustard and blue plaid shirt with short sleeves — ruffled the boy's hair a little and told him to keep the change.

Feeling good, he strutted off in the loose dirt and drank a tangy *nimboo* soda whilst smoking a Gold Leaf cigarette. *Itwaar* Bazaar could get blazing hot at high noon, situated as it was in a sprawling empty lot where the earth began to turn to sand on its way to the sea — a desert land with shifting sands. Everywhere he turned, there were women in sleeveless *shalwar kameezes* — a smorgasbord of coral pinks, henna reds, marigold oranges, glowing emerald greens — a menagerie of tropical birds.

Each one had a silken sheet of hair with one side hanging over their faces, and always, always the massive sunglasses. Javed wondered if all the rich women of Karachi knew each other and were part of a secret club with a rule that all its members wear a uniform.

The men were no different. They all had variations on a wet-looking, spiky hairstyle — talked incessantly on their mobile phones — shunning the world with equally large and bulbous shades over their eyes, ornate gold and silver logos adorning the sides.

Javed was determined to visit all the sunglass stalls — to leave no stone unturned, he was making an investment in his future, after all. He had once ventured into an eyewear shop in the urbane and hip Zamzama mercantile area. The shop was well-lit, climate-controlled and astringent — emulating a small hotel in grandeur. The guys in there *were* ordinary guys like him — but when they saw him walk in, did not attempt to disguise their lack of interest. They knew he would buy nothing.

He had seen some real beauties in there — aerodynamic as aircraft and glistening like new cars. What he hadn't been able to believe was how much the Lords and Ladies of Karachi spent on these things. 50,000 ruppees, 80,000 ruppees, one lac ruppees, one lac 50 thousand ruppees! How could this be possible? He had left the store hastily — feeling unwell and dissatisfied with everything. What hope was there for him in a world where people spent more on their eyewear than he did on his living in five years cumulatively?

Today, however, was the day he would join the cult. Granted, he would be buying knock-offs of knock-offs but he too would be safe, secure and cocooned against the world — and once that occurred who knew what was next?

As he approached one of the stalls, he noticed a young woman, in a yellow *shalwar kameez* standing by a white plastic stand of sunglasses tentatively reaching for a garish red pair of 'Gacci' shades. Her full sleeves and dupatta wrapped modestly around her person, coupled with her lack of sunglasses and skin a similar hue to his — free of make-up indicated to him a class different from all the other women, he had been seeing at the bazaar — a fact that put him at ease.

'*Yeh kitnay ka hain?*' she would ask, wait for the reply — return the pair to the stand gingerly, only to pick up another pair, try it on — peer in the mirror and then take it off and ask again:

'*Yeh kitnay ka hain?* How much are these?' As this went on for a while — Javed found himself getting impatient.

'*Behen zara hume bhi to style marney de na?*' he chided smiling, 'Sister, may I also try on some sunglasses and style myself out?'

There was something touching about the way this girl was methodically trying on the sunglasses so he resisted the temptation to turn on the Karachi-rudeness.

'*Ji?* Sorry?' She turned around startled — seeming embarrassed upon seeing him.

'Oh oh — so sorry *aiye aap aiye*. Come, please come.' She hastened to move out of the way nervously adjusting her *dupatta*. Javed felt guilty for having interrupted her.

'No, please sister,' he beckoned her back to where she had stood, 'you have spent so much time choosing — you have to at least buy a pair!' He reached over to the rack and pulled a pair off waggling them about in front of her.

She looked at her feet, '*Chaley aap pheley try kar lain phir me apna chwois bana loon ge*. It's ok — you choose first and than I'll make my choice.' Javed noted happily that she had thrown the English word 'chwois' into her speech.

He stepped forward towards the mirror and took a long, hard look at himself. He thought his face rather angular, his nose rather large and his eyebrows rather thick. He decided he definitely needed something very black and very shiny to hide his ghastly visage in.

The girl busied herself looking at the knick-knacks strewn about the tables, not wanting to be seen standing there watching him. Javed went through a few different pairs but could not for the life of him tell which suited him best or the look he wished to affect most — despite having imagined himself in a pair countless times.

He turned uncertainly to the girl in yellow and asked in broken English how he looked. She was again startled — this time, from her perusal of gee-gaws. She seemed equally uncertain how to respond. At that moment — thick curtains of oppressive societal rules and regulations that governed the interaction of men and women in public spaces — hung heavily between them.

The girl reached a decision in her head; he did not seem like a 'cheapster'. There was an earnest quality about him — a gleefullness, almost that was infectious, *and* he *had* called her 'sister' — an epithet of respect from the mouth of a Pakistani man.

'Yessss. *Ji... Ji...*' she finally nodded, adding, 'It is good one.'

Seeing the sunglasses on him made her wonder how they looked on her. She had felt like an imposter when trying them on. She saw them on the faces of the women of means who breezed laguidly everyday through the doors of the salon she worked at — getting their nails cleaned, painted & polished like buttons — their hair stringently straightened and peroxided.

Javed looked back at the mirror. Yes, these were dark and powerful enough. He pictured himself on his scooter whizzing down Boat Basin. Yes, these would do. He could almost feel the cool air conditioned breeze cooing on his skin. He motioned to the man in charge, did the prerequisite haggle tango and managed to extricate the mojo-imparting shades for 450 ruppees. They *were* worth it.

Immediately perching them on his head, he turned around.

'So what about you?' he asked his mystery co-shopper

in Urdu. She was still there waiting *patiently*, he thought, *to make her dreams too, come true*. She however, was wavering in her decision.

'*Ji me ley loon gee shukriya*. Don't worry I'll get mine.' She tried to ward Javed off, but he seemed determined. If she was going to do this, she could not deny the benefit of a male presence as the shopkeeper had been grining leerily at her since his arrival.

'Please,' Javed said beckoning her towards the mirror and rack as he stepped aside. There had been something reassuring about this figure in yellow whilst he had been choosing his sunglasses — her presence had given him a special kind of confidence. Karachi could be a lonely city for the dispossessed.

Zainab conceded and went straight for the red pair she had tried on earlier — recalling that the shopkeeper had told her they were 350 ruppees! That was a whole days tips for her and she *unlike* other women she knew did not seem to possess in her DNA (and she had tried) — the aggressive, haggling powers.

Javed looked away respectfully wanting to give her the space she required to make up for cutting in on her earlier — but upon hearing her feeble attempts to coerce the price down, he decided he owed her his services:

'*Chal chacha kum to kar*! Oh come on old man reduce the price!'

'*Nahi! Three-pipty pukka*! No it's 350 firm!'

'What are you talking about friend... 200 and not one *paisa* more!'

The man knew well he had tried to pull a fast one,

preying on a meek-looking female alone. He had not bargained for Javed showing up and ruining his prospects. Zainab looked at him expectantly. The shopkeeper frowned, twitched his moustache and said:

'Two-pipty,' in English. She hastily opened her purse pulled the requisite notes out — and handed them to him before he changed his mind.

'*Shukriya*,' she said and immediately turned to go. Javed also made to leave but the girl then turned back. She felt bad for not having thanked him.

'*Aap ka bhi shukuriya*. Thank yoo very much,' she uttered quickly. Javed was taken aback. This was the most interaction he had had with a woman in years. He managed to utter an embarrassed, 'Velcome *ji*.'

The girl then, to his (and her own) surprise — ventured on, 'I... I... have to buy more things...' she said very quickly '... for the house, if you don't mind maybe you could come along? I think I would save a great deal of money having you with me!' she exclaimed finally allowing herself to smile.

Javed was confused. He looked past her at a point in the distance and than snuck a look at her. She seemed like a decent girl. No garish make-up, no sleeveless clothes. He decided she just really wanted him to help her. She then proceeded to ask him if he ate *samosa chaat*.

'*Ji*? Sorry?' he asked utterly bewildered.

'*Samosa chaat*?' she said still smiling.

'*Ji*. Yes?' he said quickly for lack of knowing what else to say.

'Let me buy you a plate as a thank you for helping me,' she explained. She was feeling a little reckless with the coveted red sunglasses inlaid with exquisite, tiny diamantes in her possession. They walked through the loose, dusty earth in silence — shaded by the large, canvas tents that were put up every week to create the market. Javed trailed back a little. Children with unwieldly hand-woven baskets — larger than themselves kept running up to them, 'Madam please Madam 20 Rs only.' They were the porters of *Itwaar* Bazaar. Fighting and squabbling for precedence, these tiny boys and girls, barefoot and snotty-nosed — beleaguered shoppers into hiring them to carry their goods through sheer determination — children fighting to eat.

* * * * *

The heat beat down with more ferocity as it got nearer to mid afternoon. The girl felt her head getting heavy. It always did when she came here. The pungent smells, often of rotting meat from the produce and livestock section of the market pervaded the entire space.

Internally — the dust filled your nostrils and coated your throat. Externally, it stuck to the rivulets of sweat that dripped down your face. She wished she could frequent the cool and clean supermarkets of Clifton and Defence like the women she tended to in the beauty parlour. It was a mystery as to why *they* came here at all! They didn't *need* to. What was the appeal she wondered? She shook her head in disbelief at the decidedly unpredictable rich.

They ate their *Samosa chaat* in silence. The heat was slowing everything down — forcing them to conserve their energy naturally. Javed found himself drifting off to the cool of the ocean — to the beach and the seashore.

When they were finished they handed their plates back to the vendor. 'Thank you very much.... Misss...?' Javed spoke shyly realizing he did not know her name, but was too petrified to just come out and ask. He would appear out-of-line; he was sure of it. Asking for a woman's name, a stranger in a public place, was taboo.

The girl shortly realized she didn't know his name either, 'So Mr...? Now I've fed you *chaat* will you accompany me to help me with my shopping?'

'Mr. Javed *ji*. My Name is Javed.'

'Okay! Mr. Javed!' Zainab said exuberantly, 'My name is Miss Zainab,' she added the title Miss as was appropriate. She had a good feeling about 'Mr. Javed,' and could certainly use the company at the bazaar — but you never could be too careful with these men.

They spent the afternoon buying vegetables, cleaning products, and meats — Javed haggling for her at every turn. He had begun to feel quite indomitable with his sunglasses placed on his head. They had also made a firm friend in Laila — a little girl with dark eyes and matted brown hair in a filthy pink *shalwaar kameez*.

She carried the basket for them valiantly, stumbling a little as it got heavier. Zainab had said she chose her because she wanted to support female entrepreneurship even though Javed had protested saying there was no way this bird-like sprite could carry anything.

Every now and then Javed would bend down and help Laila carry the basket and she would allow him with relief. She couldn't have been more than 8 years old and had been more vociferous than her elder brothers in trying to negotiate with Zainab and Javed.

They shopped straight through high noon, taking a 7-Up break after a few hours. Javed learnt that Zainab worked at a fashionable beauty salon in Clifton and supported her whole family, including two lay-about brothers. She travelled two hours everyday from and to a *muhajir* or refugee camp on the outskirts of Karachi. She travelled on rickshaws everywhere. Javed felt surprise, alarm, but also admiration for the strange, independent ways of this woman. He did not know women like her existed. She took care of her whole family, ashamedly he was aware that even he — the eldest son did no such thing.

'Well...' said Zainab as they stood exhausted in the parking area of the bazaar, little Laila still in tow. She was now joined by her equally tiny brothers who seemed at a loose end and had decided to can the competition and instead aid their sister — possibly sharing in the dividends. 'It was very nice to meet you Mr. Javed and very nice of you to help me.' Javed shuffled his feet in the sand.

'Miss Zainab you take care of your whole family. I am glad I was able to help you'.

'Zainab,' she said impulsively.

'*Ji?*' said Javed. 'Zainab, just Zainab no need to call me Miss — after all we are equals, no?'

'Yes miss, yes miss... sorry... "Zainab",' Javed grinned, 'You are right, but...' he added sincerely, 'I wouldn't say we were equals! You are far superior!'

His candour made her laugh. It was not very often that she talked to men her age also trying to 'make it' in the big, bad city of Karachi — and certainly, never had any one of them called her superior.

Without thinking twice about it Javed pulled a little notebook from his pocket and slipped a pen off the pocket of his shirt and scribbled his number down.

'If you ever need any help again please do not hesitate to ask. Anything!' Zainab did not doubt his good intentions, and took the scrap of paper with a simple: 'Thank you.' Javed went off to hail her a rickshaw as she got embroiled in trying to sort out the wages for the day for Laila and her fellow basketeers.

* 2 *

Kareena

The evening was one of those typical of Karachi when the humidity of the day doesn't alleviate at sundown. Javed stood outside the building of the ID card office watching the dusk rolling in. His shift had just ended. Closing his eyes gratefully on his first inhale — he tugged on his Gold Leaf cigarette.

The queues lined up for their ID cards had finally dissipated. The sweat that had been dripping down all day from his scalp, onto his neck and into his clothes — whilst he sat behind the glass counter had dried into an uncomfortable film coating his body. His new plaid shirt exhibited this under his armpits. As he smoked, he waited for a breeze to come from somewhere, anywhere — to provide some relief — but tonight Karachi was at her worst.

He prepared mentally for the ride on his Vespa through the rising dust and smog, for the inevitable entrapment in the traffic on Clifton Bridge. He mused that it could be worse if he had to use the public buses — standing plastered to hundreds of people exuding the smell of the hard labour of the day. As his stomach growled, he realized it had been ages since he had eaten the greasy plate of grams for lunch.

'*Khuda Hafiz Javed*! Go with God, Javed!'

'*Khuda Hafiz Akram saab*,' Javed returned the greeting to his supervisor hastily concealing the cigarette behind his back.

'Aren't you going home?' his boss asked as he clambered into the driver's seat of his Nissan Sunny. '*Ji, Ji*. I am on my way saab,' Javed grinned sheepishly, '*Main zara huwa kha raha tha*. I was just getting some air.'

Akram Dost was the only man or woman in the *Shanaakhti* card building who had an air conditioner in his office. In the peak of the midsummer monsoon months — he very rarely even left it; ordering spicy gram curry, chicken karahi and towers of naan breads to be delivered for lunch. He always had a few of his cronies around him — drinking 7-Up in the rarefied air of the room — and now he was getting straight into his air-conditioned Nissan Sunny.

'*Yaar, kiya mazey hain*. What a life he has!' Javed mused as he watched his supervisor getting ready to head home. He imagined how he must look and cringed.

His hair was matted and greasy even though he had washed it vigorously with LifeBuoy soap this morning. He imagined he must not look much different from the grease monkeys — little boys who worked at the petrol stations changing tyres outdoors even in the peak of the afternoon in the scorching Summer months.

How cool and collected Akram Dost had looked. His white shalwar kameez was still crisp as he had walked by, releasing puffs of cool air from his voluminous clothes providing Javed with the breeze he had been hoping for, 'Aaah,' he sighed — the respite was all too brief.

'*Chaal yaar nikaltey hain*. Better get out outta here,' he thought to himself. He really did not wish to go home to his room. There was no point. It was nearing 7 o'clock and that was load-shedding time — until 10 p.m. (if lucky). If he went home, he knew he would find himself perspiring profusely in his vest and *shalwar* listening to Lata Mangeshkar on his battery-powered tape recorder, cleaning his nails by candlelight. No. Tonight he would drive to Clifton Beach

— eat a kebab roll with onions and chutney and sit on the *charpai* at the tea shop chatting with Sher Jaan, the owner.

He had waited long enough outside his office building for the traffic to subside. The day watchmen were locking up, so he got astride his China blue scooter, turned the key and urged his foot on the accelerator. 'Kareena' was his pride and joy. A gift from Moeen Chacha to help him with his new life in the big city — Moeen Chacha had coerced Kareena out of his friend who owed him some money and ran a dealership in Nazimabad. She was a little beat-up but Javed loved her. He had promptly named her Kareena because he decided the colour of the scooter resembled the eyes of Kareena Kapoor — whom he believed was the loveliest woman in Bollywood.

The scooter was what put him one rung up the ladder of hell which was life in Karachi for the have-nots. Yes, he had a pass from the nightmare of the wagons and buses. He was, however, still vulnerable to the elements and knew that he was far, far from the utter bliss of a cool, enclosed metal vestibule of joy in which to traverse the roads of Karachi — like his supervisor had. However, when he was on his scooter — at least he knew he could get where he needed to be, whenever he needed to be there.

Clifton Beach was a jovial, welcoming place any time of the day or night. As he turned off Ghazi road onto the newly tarred avenue directly in front of the beach — the lights grew brighter and the chatter of people interspersed with the laughter and squeals of children filled the air.

Smoke was rising from the multiple barbeques with sizzling meats on skewers, and couples strolled with little paper cones in their hands, popping roasted *channas* in their mouths. The restaurants were packed and hundreds of bicycles, motorcycles, taxis and cars were clustered all the way down the stretch that was the promenade. Even now, when he turned onto Beach Avenue, he got a thrill in his heart as he did when he had been a child. Moeen Chacha would drive him, his mother, father, and sister for three hours every few months inland from Nazimabad — to visit Clifton Beach for an 'outing'.

He remembered the first time he had sat in Moeen Chacha's orange Mazda. '*Eh Pappoo*,' he would love to call him by that name, 'Let me show you my *Eeyr-Condeeshuned* motor-car!' he had said picking Javed up on his shoulders and taking him over to the car.

'But Moeen Chacha — what is this *Eeyr-condeeshnr*?'

'You'll see Pappoo!'

Moeen Chacha had taken him for a drive around the block and he remembered being excited that his friends playing stick-ball in the streets would see him lording it over them in the orange Mazda with its magical '*Eyr-condeeshnur.*' He grinned recalling that maiden voyage. Moeen Chacha had turned the blower up on the vents installed in the dashboard of the car.

'Isn't the air cool huh huh?' his uncle had been smiling from ear to ear. Javed remembered experiencing a sensation of someone breathing on him... so this was the magical device his uncle had mentioned? He had been puzzled. What Javed hadn't known at the time was that Moeen Chacha actually didn't have an air-conditioner in his car.

Those who were fortunate enough to afford a motor vehicle could not always afford then to air condition them, and had only the in-built fan. Moeen Chacha had this fan, but from then till Javed was in his teens and the car eventually died, Moeen Chacha insisted it was an air conditioner

— Javed had almost believed him — so convincing was his uncle's sheer enthusiasm for feeling 'much cooler than before,' everytime he sat in that car.

Around the same time, Javed recalled, everyone in Karachi woke up to a mysterious shipwreck on Clifton Beach. One fine day, she was just there — a hulking great passenger ship beached on the shores of the Arabian Sea in urban Karachi. At first he only heard about it from the kids at school in North Nazimabad, far away from the shore. The news had spread and Javed had wished feverishly, to witness this spectre for himself — pestering Moeen Chacha to take them to the beach.

Nobody seemed to have any information about its appearance — but within days it had been explored by looters, buccaneers and highwaymen hoping to find treasures.

Perhaps they did. The ship remained. There was nothing about it in the newspapers, certainly nothing on the television. Javed only remembered one state-owned television channel — Pakistan Television that endlessly recounted stories of this minister meeting that minister or the glory of the army.

No-one tried to move the ship. Parts of it disintegrated and fell off. Children played around it. For 20 odd years the ship stayed rotting away until just as suddenly as it had arrived, it was gone. As Javed pulled up into the parking area of the beach that evening — in his imagination the ship of his childhood was still there. It would always be there — that and the pungent aroma of dead fish.

Clifton Beach was no beauty. The sands were verging on the black side of grey, with muck piled up everywhere. Slimy hills of seaweed, old shoes, dog excrement, human excrement, oil slicks and pieces of glass adorned the shores —

this was no encouragement to walk barefoot and yet people did. Tonight Javed walked right onto the beach craving the cool sands under his feet — the all-encompassing sound of the waves raging in his ears. Since the big sell-out of Clifton Beach to the Arabs, all kinds of improvements had taken place. There were giant floodlights illuminating everyone's activities, benches now; attempts to keep the area clean had been made, attempts that seemed to fail.

Javed rolled up his trousers — took off his *Bata* chappals and holding them in one hand, headed towards the waters lapping at the shore — walking for what seemed like hours. His trousers got soaked but he felt invigorated having washed off the frustrations of a day in Karachi — bathing in the holy waters of her Ganga.

'*Eh Sher Jaan ji*! *Khanaa mil jai ga*? Hello Sher Jaan! Can I get some food?'

Javed approached his mustachioed friend Sher Jaan squatting over the rim of a giant clay oven expertly slapping wet dough onto the insides of the orange, glowing cavity. His younger brother Athar Jaan, on the other side of the assembly line, then deftly removed the freshly baked *naan* bread with a long iron rod hooked at the end. The operation required a great deal of expertise for it to move efficiently. Sher Jaan had been doing this for 30 years — and proudly proclaimed that he had never yet lost a *naan* to the fires of the *tandoori*. The aroma of the hot *naans* filled the air and Javed's stomach emitted an audible rumble.

'*Arey Javed! Kiya holia banna rakha he yaar*? Javed my boy — look at the state of you?' Sher Jaan remarked with concern, 'Come, come sit. Why were you roaming the seashore like a man who has lost his lover! You should at least eat first!' his voice boomed loud and deep — echoing through, in the *tandoori* whilst his face glowed in the light of its fires.

This was the warm hearth of Javed's life. Sher Jaan was like a father in this crazy city of Karachi — showing concern as he did, about Javed's health, happiness and above all lack of moustache.

He insisted that Javed must grow a moustache not unlike his own bristling Punjabi specimen. He would proudly twirl it on either end whilst musing under the stars over a cup of *cha* at the end of a long night serving the hoardes of Karachi at Clifton Beach.

'*Much nahi te kuch nahi saeen*! If you have no moustache, you have nothing my son!' he would boom at Javed. 'You just grow one. You'll see! You'll become a man!'

Javed would listen politely nodding his head at Sher Jaan, but he was sure that a moustache such as the one Sher Jaan wanted him to cultivate needed an entirely different species of man to carry it off. He was too lanky, his hair was a thick black thatch (that he carefully coiffered every day with Brylcreem, mind) — he preferred English-style shirts and trousers to *shalwaar kameez* and his skin, he decided was the colour of *nihari* — the traditional Pakistani meat stew.

'So brother have your dreams come any closer?' Sher Jaan's brother — the thinner, younger version of the elder also with vigorous moustache but quiet demeanour — asked him.

'No brother. I am pretty much the same as when I last spoke to you,' Javed replied.

'But you wear the English clothes. You ride the English scooter. Have you learnt actual English yet or no?' Athar

Jaan asked him. Many a night, Javed had sat late with them, sometimes serious, sometimes jesting, about a time when he too would walk the English walk and talk the English talk.

Once, when he was 18, he had come to the city with his friends and they were hanging out by Mr Burger at Boat Basin when a gleaming white car had rolled up in front of them. The windows tinted a lustrous black allowed none to view the precious cargo inside. The driver was wearing a crisp, white military-style uniform complete with a hat dressed with gold brocade. He honked impatiently for service.

Within minutes, at Boat Basin — any car driving up, was certain to have at least eight waiters from the surrounding restaurants bear down on it very much like a swarm (masses of flies were also present in any case). *Mezbaan, Balouch Ice Cream, Flamingo Chaat*, all were represented in a bidding war. One had to know exactly what one craved and from where.

If you appeared particularly wealthy, unscrupulous waiters would often trick you into believing they were from the place you wanted them to be from but would actually work for a less reputable establishment. So much of the food was almost identical, they would sometimes get away with it — or have to take the hit, if the person cottoned-on. This night was no different.

In response to the driver's honking, a small battalion of waiters — little boys and girls begging or selling flowers *and* begging all descended upon the car — the driver obviously well-versed in the protocol, quickly ascertained who was actually from his ward's desired choice of restaurant, placed his order, and rudely bellowed the rest away. That was when the black window rolled down and Javed saw a woman so stunning in appearance — he did fall over.

She was wearing a sleeveless red *kameez* with copper embroidery — her bare arms glowing gold in the luminous hues of the setting sun. Her hair he remembered to be of a superior gloss — deep red and lustrous. Her eyes were obscured by the largest, blackest pair of sunglasses Javed had ever seen — the oversized gold emblems embroidering the sides reminding Javed of the gold seals of Mughals.

She had leaned out of the window and gestured out towards Javed, waving an immaculate hand adorned with gold bangles, chunky rings and nails glinting a sharp, ruby red whilst alternately scolding her driver: 'ABBAS, I told you I wanted the *chaat* without the crispy topping! Why didn't you tell him? You idiot!' Javed had not known what to do and had started coming forward, only to be pushed away by the obnoxious driver, 'Not you! You fool. Him!' Behind Javed, the waiter was walking over uncertain what he was getting himself into.

Javed was mortified. The woman in red leaned over to her companion, speaking in English that Javed could not fully catch. Their ensuing laughter, although light felt sharp — like splinters of fine glass. Abbas the driver was both apologizing profusely to her *and* yelling at the waiter. The window slowly rolled back up leaving a void in Javed's sight. Inside, the occupants of the car sat protected — from the thrum of black flies, population of beggars, Karachi dust, possibly him and the scorching rays of the sun.

He often revisited what she may have said to her friend that day. The feeling of inadequacy he experienced in that moment flared up sometimes.

* 3 *

Javed

Zainab was unable to stop thinking about her eventful day with Javed. He had seemed genuinely concerned about her getting swindled by unscrupulous sales people. She realized for her even such a small modicum of caring was more than she could remember having felt in a long time.

She tucked the groceries they had bought together away in the cupboards of the tiny kitchen — feeling lighter than when she had left the house that morning.

It was a crowded house Zainab lived in with four immediate family members and four other relatives.

Her brothers had not come home the night before, and her mother had been in a state.

'Amma! I have to go to *Itwaar* Bazaar. I don't know why you're getting into such a frenzy over your darling sons!' she yelled at her mother who was wringing her hands and beating her chest, 'They do this all the time, and you know full well they're probably lying in a drug induced stupour somewhere, and will be home when they regain consciousness,' Zainab had no patience left for her brothers.

She didn't *have* to go to *Itwaar* Bazaar. In fact, she had to do the lengthy journey into town every day and would rather not have to on her day off. But it was necessary to get out of the house, and despite the heat and dust of the market which she loathed — it was an escape. Her mother would be fine. Once she had squeezed every last drop of melodrama out of herself — she would fall asleep on her *charpai*. Then her brothers would come slinking in sheepishly looking like hell. Her mother would wake up instantly, and start yelling and screaming at them, beating them and the melodrama would begin again.

Zainab would return after they had made peace. Her brothers squatting, silently drinking tea and her mother getting ready to make the evening's *chapattis*. It never varied, except that evening when she got home, her elder brother looked worse than usual — sporting a black eye and a gash in his cheek. 'What happened Kamran? Did your drug dealer beat you up because you couldn't pay him?' she asked coolly.

'Maybe if you gave me more money he wouldn't have to,' her brother replied gruffly.

'You're disgusting,' said Zainab, without remorse.

'Oh yes and you're so high-and-mighty, with your fancy job aren't you. You're no better than a servant — remember that! Rubbing and pressing the feet of those fat bitches!'

Zainab said nothing — looking at her mother who carried on making her *chapattis*. '*Haan haan Amma*. Yes, Yes — mother let him talk to me any way he wants. One of these days I will be gone and then what will all of you do?' she said finally. Her mother looked up at her with a haunted look in her eyes, 'We'll die. What else?'

Unable to be around them any longer Zainab went back indoors to the room that she called her own. That was the one thing she had put her foot down about. If she was going out and working — one of the few rooms of the house had to be hers and hers alone. The rest of them would just have to figure it out. She entered and switched on the naked light bulb that hung loosely in the centre of the ceiling. To her disgust, her other brother, Imran, was lying in her bed, flat on his stomach — one leg hanging over the edge. Drool escaped his mouth. She shook him violently — calling his name, but he was in so deep a sleep that he barely registered her vehement attempts to rouse him. He groaned, but didn't shift a muscle.

Exasperated, she sat on the edge of the bed, her handbag still hanging from her shoulder. Her thoughts turned to the day's events again and the kindness of the man she had met, Javed. She pulled the sunglasses out from her bag, turning them over in her hands marvelling at their beauty. She examined the piece of paper that Javed had scribbled his number on. He really was earnest when he had offered himself for any assistance she may need. Would she actually ever call him? How could she? Wouldn't it be wrong? He said that he wanted to help her, and she was surprised at how easily she believed him. Her brother emitted another groan and she kicked his dangling leg lightly with her foot, disliking his presence.

She stood up, placing her new sunglasses onto a small, wooden dressing table next to a turquoise blue tin of Tibet Snow talcum powder, an ancient wooden hairbrush, tweezers and thread, two rusty tubes of Swiss Miss lipstick (which she had owned for longer then she remembered) and hardly-used Hashmi surma for her eyes.

The sunglasses struck an odd chord with the assortment of antiquated accessories—glistening and shiny—positing possibilities for Zainab.

Through the walls she could hear her father's brother yelling at his wife — their children crying. Her own father was unwell and frail, constantly sleeping in the room the rest of her family shared.

His brother was a cruel and selfish man, who had

insisted on them living together to help take care of their family but actually did nothing for them, often trying to get away with not paying the rent. Zainab had to regularly fight battles with the man.

She realized she was exhausted, and rolled out an old mattress on the floor to prepare to go to sleep. She couldn't be bothered trying to get Imran out of her room. He would wake up at some time in the wee hours and slink out himself, most likely to find another fix.

She picked up the piece of paper with Javed's number on it and folded it carefully, placing it in an inside pocket of her purse. She got her clothes ready for work the next day — thankful that she had that to look forward to.

4

Systems Of Control

Javed was having a terrible day. It was the first week of July, and was proving to be the hottest day — so far — of the year. From behind his plexiglass shield he watched the scores of people from the outerlying rural areas, or from bungalows in Kehkashan — lining up outside, waiting impatiently to get their new identity cards. It was a government initiative started in the early 2000s. After being children of chaos it was proving extraordinarily difficult for the citizens of Pakistan to adapt to any form of order, such as the ID card inferred.

Many believed that it was pushed on Pakistan by the Americans. 'How could it not be?' Javed had heard his colleagues say at lunch. Ayaaz one of the senior clerks a well-educated, fiery man to whom everyone looked up, argued that it had occurred right after 9/11 making their lives and sundry more difficult under the guise of making them easier — how most regulation-making and innovations in technology in the West, he believed, operate.

'They are all predicated on an idea of ease or order, but more often than not are a system of control!'

System of control or not, Javed's head was pounding — and he was sick of trying to explain to person after person what documents they needed to get an ID card, and facing blank incomprehension.

'Photooos? We need photos?'

'Yes, you need photos. Come back when you have photos.'

'But my father's brother's uncle's cousin's roommate is

the Governor of XYZ?'

'Well you still need an ID card, and yes you will have to wait here and get it done yourself.'

The standard Pakistani operational mode of the upper echelon angered Javed no end. Nepotism, favouritism, bribes, corruption were rampant and being a servant of the civil service Javed had to encounter it pretty much on a daily basis. He believed the instatement of the ID card was the first great leveller in Pakistani society.

For the first time, it had become challenging for the elite classes to palm a chore off on their peons. They actually had to make an appearance at the I.D card office and it pissed them off no end. Javed watched not entirely without a modicum of glee, the young kids scowling in the queue with their pre-requisite escorts, shades wrapped supportively around their heads.

They didn't seem to have any idea what the rest of the country, nay, the city of Karachi itself endured. They behaved like they were deities — accustomed to the rarefied air of their abodes, unable to breathe the air if they had to step out. A man in a white high collared jacket, white trousers and a stiff peaked white navy hat with an officious air about him came up to the counter and said:

'*Dekhey merey baba ki burri haalaat ho rahee hain garrmee say. Vo udhr garree me betha hain.* Look my 'baba'/ward is in a terrible state because of the heat. He's sitting over there in the car,' indicating a flame red Honda Civic. Through the moderately tinted windows Javed spied a haughty looking young boy with black spiky hair sitting on the back seat — eyes glued to something that looked like a phone but was larger than one.

'Why don't you just give me the form and let him stay in the car ai?' said the man waggling his eyebrows at Javed in a meaningful way.

The perspiration was dripping down Javed's back almost in time to the red second hand of the standard government issue — white clock in the office. The air had steadily gotten thicker with the foul odour of human sweat. He looked at this pompous little man — a slave no doubt to the family he worked for, ready to do anything to serve them — bobbing his head day and night: Yes Sir, No Sir, Three bags Full Sir. Javed came across hundreds of men like this all day — every day, some more obnoxious than others. Than he looked over at Mr. Malcontent in his cool climate-controlled envelope, and wanted to scream.

'Sir', he replied with a sharpness that could cut glass, 'Your ward has legs yes? Hands and feet? Can't you see how many people are standing here? Don't you think they too are suffering in the heat? If he wants the ID card than 'your baba,' will have to move those hands and feet and come over here!'

He could have let the damn brat sit in his car and let the mustachioed idiot do the running around, but he was just not in the mood today to pander to the whims of those much, much more fortunate than him.

* * * * *

Javed made his first solo trip into the city without the family, when he was 14 with a posse of school friends and their elder brothers. They had planned to come in from Nazimabad, doubling and tripling up on the five motorbikes they had between 12 of them. They caroused around Boat Basin and loitered at Clifton Beach but the highlight of the trip was their visit to the glassy, imposing newly constructed Park Towers Mall in the heart of Clifton. The guards at the doors had given them some grief. Single men in packs in Karachi were not welcome everywhere — particularly at these harbours of wealth.

Javed had walked into the mall after the long motorbike journey riding pillion on the handlebars, and had been struck dumbfounded. The smell of rotting fish — a familiar smell in Karachi was absent, and a breeze so bracing it chilled him to the core was blowing directly on his face. He turned to his friends incredulously and said, '*Yaar ye jannat ki hawa kahan say aa rahee hain*? Man where is this heavenly breeze coming from?' They ridiculed him and Rashid had told him with a worldly-wise flourish '*Yeh hain The Mall kaa kamaal Baboo! The Mall kaa kamal*! This is the wonder of the Mall, friend... The Mall!'

Anjum put his arm around Javed's shoulder, stating with mock-solemnity:

'Velcome to Janat *bhai*! Velcome to Paradise, brother.' They had not been able to purchase a single item at the mall that day — the only thing that they had bought were little paper cups of spiced corn kernels to share called Magic Corn. Even those were 60Rs each... an upmarket version of the wares of the street hawker. Nonetheless, they had hung around the mall for hours going round and about in circles taking in the sights, the sounds and above all relishing the blessed relief from the hot day.

11 years later Javed was still chasing his beloved 'heavenly breeze'. When he first moved to Karachi, he visited the malls avidly. He had also obsessively visited as many air conditioner showrooms as he could possibly find. He was struck by something strange. The air-conditioner shops

never actually had air conditioners running; they were more like auto parts shops. The Gizri shopping area was full of them. He had found out every price and model available. He determined he would need 35,000 ruppees just to purchase the least expensive 1 ton A/C — a small affair nothing like the split level A/Cs (veritable powerhouses of air conditioning that the very rich installed for maximum coolness). Size, however, Javed learnt didn't matter if there was no electricity for at least 4-6 hours every day — peaking at 8-10 hours when it got *really* bad.

Much to Javed's dismay it was then that the rich and *very* rich realized they had to now buy *mammoth* electrical generators in order to power their air conditioners, which went for upwards from 60,000 ruppees, with the most expensive one at 150,0000 ruppees. On top of the initial expense, petrol, an expensive fuel, was required to run it. All in all, Javed determined a little downcast, that it was an absurd and altogether mystifying state of affairs.

He soon worked out that even if he could afford an air conditioner he would need an extra 6,000 ruppees every month just to pay for the electricity (when there was electricity). A catch-22. Of course he imagined he would be prudent. He would put it on for an hour at night and then switch it off — ingeniously using the fan's movement to circulate the cool air. He would close all the windows.

Yes, Javed decided he too would have his cocoon world. However, whilst he was sitting in the 7th circle of hell at his workplace that afternoon — Javed was entirely uncertain that the existence he desired so ardently would ever be his.

∗ 5 ∗

'Armane'

Javed's old buddies from home — Haris, Anjum and Rashid — had declared it was time for all of them to get together. They rung incessantly — all day Saturday until he answered the phone.

As a rule, he tried to avoid them; he felt they were juvenile, spendthrifts who only cared about '*poondi*', — whereas for him there was nothing more embarrassing and alarming than driving around watching and pestering women — even merely the word *poondi* made him cringe. But it had been a while since he had seen them and he had been a little lonely — so he agreed to meet for a meal of Student Bhiryani, a Karachi institution, after work.

The breeze from the Arabian ocean was blowing inland that night, making it a bearable evening. Javed cruised over to Tariq road, and pulled up outside Student Bhiryani — where they served an array of spicy rice pilafs. The gang was all there hanging out on their bikes, cracking jokes loudly.

'*Eh chichoray*! Hey you loiterer!' Javed yelled out teasing — hoping to get Anjum's attention as he walked over to them.

'Oi hoi! Oi hoi! Look who's coming over!' His friends spontaneously began to heckle and jeer upon spying Javed.

'*Kidhr reh jatta hain yaar*? Where do you disappear to man?' Haris asked. They all wondered what Javed did with his time since he didn't spend much time with them. They knew he didn't have a girlfriend — he didn't have the nerve to befriend a girl, let alone have a 'girlfriend'.

'*Buss yaar*. Not much man,' Javed uttered non-committally, '*Kaam shaam Yeh vo*. Work-Shirk. This'n'that.'

They sat at the rickety tables placed outside Student Bhiryani — primarily a delivery place — eating up and drinking Apple Sidra, reliving old times. Haris worked in a cellular phone company as a clerk, Anjum at a television studio as a cameraman. He hoped to work his way up to a commercials director some day.

Rashid, the most philosophical of Javed's friends worked in the most unlikeliest of places — a very expensive designer clothing store near Ideal Bakery, in a posh part of Karachi. It was the kind of store that sold handbags made by Western designers for upwards of one lac ruppees. Rashid often marvelled at the strangeness of the world that he was privy to by working there. Previously, he had not imagined the extent to which, despite the amount of poverty in the nation — the urban centres particularly Karachi, were teeming with label-loving socialites.

To Rashid's mind Karachi had a rather incongruous, surreal visual landscape unlike the Western cities, he saw in American films — where the differences between rich and poor are not always immediately detectable. Outside the store he worked in, beggars with tattered clothing and no shoes, obviously desperate for nutrition, would cluster around the large, hunking great shiny cars of his customers; men at the wheel sporting authentic Armani shirts that cost 32,000 ruppees each — a sum the beggars could not even in wildest dreams conceive one man's shirt costing. Their wives, sported Chanel sunglasses and Mulberry handbags that they purchased during their latest vacation abroad. He would overhear them talking of places with names such as 'High Street Kensington', 'Bloomys,' 'Selfridges,' 'Harrods'.

The guys exchanged stories about their jobs. Anjum was excited about the work his channel was doing. He loved to talk of how the media had grown exponentially since the 90s to an extent that no-one could ever have predicted for Pakistan. He got frustrated, however, that cameramen were akin to the runners of the Western TV and film industry. He complained that they made next to no money despite their skill-set and had very little chance of moving up. He did, however, get to see beautiful and wholly inaccessible models and actresses from time to time, which made his job the most glamorous in the eyes of his friends.

Rashid was animated that evening.

'These regular customers of mine were talking about a party in Korangi *yaar*!' All of them had heard the rumours — about these 'new' types of parties in Karachi. They apparently took place in odd places like old unused warehouses out in an area (Korangi) that no self-respecting socialite would ever have previously found themselves in. Raves had come to Pakistan... Karachi style — a little less heart'n'soul and a little more fashion and trend; not so much about the music, and say the ecstacy, as an excuse to party (although the ecstacy had found its way there too; about a decade after the U.K.).

This party had Rashid excited. His customers who had taken a shine to him had said they would put him and his buddies on the guest list if he wanted.

'*Nai yaaaar*! No way maaan,' Haris nearly fell off his chair exclaiming, 'All of us? Really? All our names? How can this be?'

Rashid just smiled, winking at Haris confidently. Javed was nonplussed. 'Who the hell is going to drive all the way out to Korangi?' Petrol was expensive. Javed didn't believe they would be allowed in, guest list or no guest list.

The raves were strictly policed and controlled, organized by big-time socialites — industrialists, business men sometimes even drug dealers — and tickets were set high enough to keep the proletariat out, thus ensuring the presence of *only* the elite. They were sold solely through word-of-mouth. For single, not-so hip guys (like them, Javed thought) not born with the proverbial silver spoon, attendance at these parties was a fanciful flight. They had never known where to begin to sniff out tickets.

Besides which, they had absolutely no chance of any females accompanying them — and everyone knew the rules changed if one had female companions. It guaranteed entry. Due to the restrictions on women's movements — most parties ended up being all-male affairs usually ending in brawls and gun-slinging. Rashid had told him that by 3 a.m. you could stake your life on it that some drunken, feudal's son would decide it was time to take offence to just about anything, or nothing and pull a gun out of his pocket (that he took with him everywhere he went) and shoot it into the air.

Javed remembered standing outside, just hoping to get into things like this for hours with about a hundred other guys. It was degrading. Especially when immaculately groomed denizens of Karachi glided right by, looking like they didn't want to walk too close to them.

He recalled one comment in particular that a husky-voiced woman dressed in sleek black, sparkling with silver sequins had made:

'*Hai Jaani dekho kitnay chichorey kharey hain*. Darling, Look how many losers are standing in line!'

' *Fikr nai karo un ko undr thorri aaney dey gey*. Don't worry they're hardly going to be let in,' her well-dressed (and Javed thought rather oily) companion had reassured her.

He remembered the expression on her face — one of sheer terror — as she had looked back over her shoulder to check that the undesirables were not in fact following her in. Javed remembered at that moment realizing how great the divide was between Him and His kind and Them and Their kind.

'But I'm not dressed man!' Haris said pragmatically. 'Let's go to Zainab Market and get some t-shirts,' Rashid suggested. 'You're mad,' Javed enjoined weakly, sensing himself being lured into the herd. He figured he had nothing else going on so what the hell? They had never actually got into any of these things, so it was win-win if a miracle occurred and they did.

* * * * * *

On the way over to shop for T-shirts, Javed envisioned the good old days, when in a posse they would drive around on their motorbikes — now less a few, going nowhere, yet going everywhere. Eating *paans*, smoking cigarettes — what else was there to do after all. Javed always felt a twinge of nostalgia when he saw the motorcycle 'crews' in Karachi, still a common sight, especially late at night.

Always all-male, now more rowdy than he remembered them to be, shouting and screaming, harassing solitary cars on the road. When he and his cohorts had engaged in this pastime, they never meant any harm, Javed mused — they were just a bunch of guys letting off steam, nothing else to do, nowhere else to go. No clubs, no bars, a few rickety cinemas, and next to no avenues to casually meet the opposite sex, that is — Javed thought, not entirely without acrimony — if you were one of those people who had *not* gone to expensive private schools, did *not* eat at the few trendy gentrified restaurants in Karachi and did not shop at Zamzama for a party. If you did, mind, there were parties like these — exclusive members-only clubs; a whole world of wonders.

'*But I did meet a girl*,' Javed contemplated his chance encounter with Zainab. He recalled her look of silent triumph when she finally procured the red shades and smiled to himself. He felt he knew exactly what she had felt. An image, unbidden of him and Zainab on his Vespa came to him. He brushed it aside, for at the moment — he had Haris clinging to him, chittering away in his ear, whilst Javed tried his best to hear above the roar of the traffic all around.

The other two were riding pillion on Anjum's motorbike — careening and swerving in between the speeding cars, animal-driven carts, mammoth whale-sized processional trucks, ramshackle Suzuki vans with drivers of dubious talent — and other equally motivated motorcyclists on a Saturday evening in Karachi.

Haris had a friend who manned a stall in Zainab Market, the hub for rejected Western garments found wanting for export purposes, but accepted with their flaws by the locals.

The market was Karachi legend growing over decades from strength to strength, as all manner of Karachi-ites flocked there to buy their t-shirts, cargo trousers, cotton nighties and all other ready-mades that could not be procured elsewhere. The rich came here in order to be amused at being able to purchase about 10 items for 1000 ruppees or so and the less rich to have access to Western clothing at Eastern prices.

When Haris walked up to his friend's stall the young man's face lit up and he immediately went for an embrace. He was dressed in purple pants with rip-cords and a yellow T-shirt with the words 'ARMANE' emblazoned on the front.

'Haris *Bhai*!' he greeted him warmly. They had been close in the old neighbourhood in North Nazimabad, his elder brother, had been Haris's classmate — so he *was* like a *bhai*. Haris aimiably ruffled the boy's hair, 'How are you Chintoo?'

Chintoo, or Tariq proceeded to pull out — what to his mind were t-shirts that epitomized cool — to help the guys out. Chintoo believed he was an authority on what the fashionable set of Karachi wore, after all they came to him every day! After much hilarity and joshing, four t-shirts were chosen. Anjum had chosen a black t-shirt, because in the films and shows he had seen about America the people in the media — particularly the directors, always wore black. His t-shirt read: GET, printed in the same style as a GAP logo. Rashid, the best-looking amongst them had opted for a red t-shirt under Tariq's instruction because it, 'set his hazel eyes off' — a remark that had made all the guys snicker.

Chintoo might have been gay but he was akin to a younger brother to Haris, so no-one made any untoward comments. Javed had decided on a black t-shirt too, and Haris had chosen a dark blue T-shirt that had the words 'Professional' printed on the back and nothing else to indicate why the words were there or what they referred to. Chintoo had done his best to persuade Haris into wearing a pastel blue T-shirt but to no avail.

It was a glorious evening, as they rode the breeze towards Korangi in anticipation of the promise the night held. When they arrived it was a sight to behold. Honda Civics and Pajeros were parked in a scattered array along the side of the road — a steady thumping was discernible, up through the bowels of the ground getting louder and clearer every time the main door opened to permit a charmed one to enter. More cars and jeeps were pulling up by the minute.

Rashid gesticulated wildly at a large black Pajero that had just parked, 'Look! Look! How many babes there are in that car!' The car was laden with girls. Four in the back, one in the passenger seat leaning over to talk to her friends in the back, who were waving cigarettes around. Javed wondered how the guy in the driver's seat with hair that looked like it was glued in place had managed to bring five girls with him. But then again he did have that shiny, black Pajero.

The gates to the warehouse were large imposing iron sheets. Guards with large moustaches in grey *shalwar kameezes*, red berets and guns slung around their shoulders stood in front of them. As per usual, hoardes and hoardes of guys just like them unaccompanied by females, hung around outside in the hopes that they might get in. The guards were having none of it. Javed shook his head — admiring at the same time their regrettable determination.

'What's up man?' Rashid asked him.

'Nothing, man. You do realize they're never letting us in.' Rashid just smacked Javed's arm lightly saying, 'You're a fool!' He seemed to have an unshakeable faith in the fact that his name would be duly included on the sacred guest list just as his customers had promised him — after all he had given them massive discounts! The girls from the black Pajero and the dude with them walked right by Javed.

He noticed the girls, this time in a different 'style' but yet still all assuming a uniform of a kind — identical tight jeans and sleeveless t-shirts, straight shiny sheaths of hair swinging as they walked. He recalled that whilst talking about her work Zainab had mentioned something about how there was no way of knowing if a woman in Karachi had naturally curly hair for they had any kink blow-dried out of existence. He wondered if Zainab had anything to do with their hair this evening.

Anjum grabbed Javed's arm, 'Come here man. Stop daydreaming!' 'What's up?' Javed asked. Anjum commandeered him round the corner to the empty lot next to the warehouse which was bathed in darkness. Rashid and Haris were walking up to the gate and did not notice as the two ducked out.

'This!' Anjum said, waving what looked like a cigarette with a twisted end in Javed's face.

'Noo man,' Javed declined the joint. He hadn't smoked hash in ages and the last time he had scarcely been able to stand.

Anjum insisted. 'I swear I didn't put much in it! C'mon *yaar*! If we do get in — it will be great to be stoned and if we don't then at least we'll *be* stoned!'

Unable to argue with that logic, Javed gave in, after all it was one of those nights where caution was resolutely flung to the wind.

* 6 *

On The Wings Of An Angel

The hash smelt and tasted great. 'We better hurry,' Javed said, 'The guys will freak out'. Just as he spoke, his mobile rang — handing Anjum the joint, he answered it. 'Yep. Yep. We're coming *yaar*. We're just around the corner. Anjum had to do Number 1. Yeah, yeah... we're coming — we're coming man!'

As he they walked back over to the madness, Javed felt relaxed and couldn't control the grin on his face. Anjum gave him a look as if to say, 'What did I tell you?' The colours of the lights adorning the exterior walls of the warehouse looked brighter. The faces of the hoardes of hopefuls had blurred, and the thumping seemed louder and more insistent. Perhaps tonight *was* the night.

'Come on, come on man, come on!' Haris grabbed their arms impatiently, as they approached the gate where he had been waiting for them.

'What's the matter man. Where's the fire?' Anjum asked lazily also unable to keep from smiling. '*Arey saaley charsi dono*. You stoned idiots, don't you know?' Haris replied knowing exactly where the two of them had been and what they were doing, 'Rashid is inside! He's waiting for us *yaar*!'

* * * * * *

It was like a dream that he had never had, for only dreams could be like this. There appeared to be at least a million people in this expansive warehouse space. More coloured lights artfully sat in every corner like at the celebrations at Abdullah Shah Ghazi's shrine every Thursday night — except this room was filled with beautiful women and was much cleaner. Above all there was a music like he had never heard before.

It pounded through to the core of him in a rhythmic kathak with his heart. His eyes were watering from the perpetual flashing of colours, his ears full of sound. This was beyond his wildest imagination. The women were full of abandon and joy dancing in groups with other women *and* men. They all looked like they knew exactly what they were doing there and why.

Rashid turned to him and said,

'What did I tell you? Huh huh?' and Javed had to do a double-take because Rashid's teeth were glowing an unearthly glow.

'What happened to your teeth man?' he asked alarmed. Rashid laughed heartily.

'It's the lighting! Your teeth look pretty scary too!'

'Really?' Javed looked around noticing that all the whites in the massive warehouse were this ethereal blue colour. The four of them worked their way through the jostling crowds with Rashid at the head. He found a nook that was not populated so they could sit and re-group — overtaken as they were by the shock of actually being allowed in.

'So brothers?' Smiling, Anjum looked at each one of his friends.

'This is it!' He had procured a tube that was lit up green by no discernible electrical source and waved it in their faces. Javed noticed many of the party-goers were sporting similar instruments in electric pinks, smouldering reds, glowing blues and fluorescent yellows — waving them around as they danced. Some particularly gifted souls, he observed, were creating intricate and energetic movements with these objects, causing Javed to feel like he was hallucinating. With the hashish coursing through his blood he wondered if he actually was.

'Brother at least keep your mouth from hanging open!' Haris put his hand under Javed's chin and gently pushed upwards. Javed turned his head slowly to look at him and then looked right back at the spectacle of movement and lights.

Was this then his entrance into the lush forbidden entrance of Paradise? he wondered. Anjum came over and sat down next to him putting his arm across Javed's shoulder. He nodded at him, equally stoned and elated as if to say: *this is our night.* Shortly, Haris came running up to them excitedly, 'I've brought us something,' he said mysteriously with his hands clasped behind his back.

Javed had no idea what he was talking about. Haris squeezed into an inconspicuous corner and somehow above the noise and the din and the hysteria of the night it was communicated that he had procured '*jadoo vali davai*' or the medicine of magic.

He had mentioned it a few times over the years, expressing a desire to get his hands on some. It was rumoured to make you feel like an eagle soaring in the skies — happier, lighter, *freer.*

The guys had naturally laughed at him. None of them had ever been into drugs or alcohol in any serious kind of way. But here he was on this most inexplicable night with two white tablets in the palm of his hand the word: 'Professional' glowing in that unearthly white-blue glow on his t-shirt.

There was no question about it. The pills were broken in half and each of them downed the glistening semi-circles.

* * * * * *

There was he — Javed moving his arms and legs and head like he had never moved them before. There was Anjum next to him with a smile that could fill the sky. Haris with his arms up in the air and Rashid in his red t-shirt like a bronze Adonis was shaking his hips with two girls on either side. Javed's heart was filling the room. He could not stop his mouth from stretching in a grin to the point where it was starting to ache.

He did not know what was going on but he was in love: with the world; with these people; with his friends. Strangers kept smiling at him and he back at them as if they had known each other for several lifetimes. He thought some faces looked familiar, from T.V., or from the glossy magazines in English he flicked through but never bought — and they were looking at him, dancing next to him — smiling at him.

The lights were pulsing brighter. Javed was starting to feel unfathomably hot. His own voice was reciting his poetry to him:

Khuwahish hain siraf itni / My deepest wish is not considerable.

Key iss kaafir jiss ko janat kabhi na miley gee / Let this sinner who shall never be blessed with heaven.

Kabhi na pai ga / Never gain entrance.

Iss zindagaan me janat ki huwa khaaney dey / In this brief lifetime, let me experience that heavenly breeze.

He mouthed the words to himself *janat ki huwa* a few times. Yes, he thought to himself — *Tu to puhanch giya bhai ya.* You have arrived brother, you have arrived. You are on the threshold of paradise. He saw something move in the corner of his eye. Was it an angel? Yes, it was an angel. It was Kareena. It had to be Kareena. It was Kareena. He moved towards the figure. She kept moving. He worked his way through the throngs, more glowing white teeth, more smiles and he found himself at the door to the outside world and walked through it.

And then — it was cold. There was light in the sky — surely, when he had entered it had been dark? His vision was blurring and flickering like bad reception on the television. From utter joy, he felt a chill in his heart and stumbled over to a small patch of grass. He lay down on his back.

He was shivering. He sat up and his stomach did a swirl and before he knew what was happening Javed was vomiting unceremoniously in the grass. Then everything went black.

* * * * * *

'*Kareena, Kareena Meree hoor pari.* Kareena Kareena My Angel of Heaven,' Javed was mumbling incoherently.

'Oi!' Haris was trying to wake him from his stupour, and then louder, 'Oi! *Javed ke bachey*!'

Javed felt his eyelids slide into his sockets to reveal his eyeballs to the world. He stared blankly at the faces of Anjum, Rashid and Haris crowded over him, with a few sundry people clustered around behind them.

'Hehe,' he started to laugh, 'hehehe,' then his head started to pound and he felt like he was going to lose his stomach lining again, and sure enough he did.

'*Haan haan aur huss salley aur huss hume to dara diya na! Haram zadey!* Yes, yes laugh it up you bastard! Scared the hell out of us didn't you?' said Anjum vociferously.

Javed looked back up at his friends after leaning over to the side for a few minutes. They looked a little rough he decided. What had happened? There had been Kareena. He remembered that... and lights... but oh right now physically, mentally — emotionally he felt like someone who had attempted suicide by jumping off a building — and survived — so totally shit and a little stupid.

'Let's get out of here guys,' he grunted reaching his hand out to Rashid to help him up, 'Let's get the hell out of here.'

Haris asked the pragmatic question, 'But can any of us drive?'

Rashid looked over at Javed, 'Well? Can you?'

'I don't know?'

Haris looked at Anjum, 'Can you?'

'I don't know! But he definitely can't!' Anjum said pointing at Javed.

The mood was alleviated as they all burst into laughter.

'You bastards. Stop it! Ohhh my head give me some freakin' water sister-fucker,' Javed realized he was thirstier than he had ever been in his entire life, and the light was absolutely blinding him.

All the party-goers leaving looked like victims of some major catastrophe going off to the hospital — some slumped against others for support to help them walk, some with hair standing on end.

Two girls had black tear-streaked faces and were shuffling out sheepishly, but all of them — all of them still had sunglasses firmly established on their faces or heads.

Javed watched in wonder and had an epiphany. This must be why they always always wore sunglasses, he decided — as he realized much to his great disappointment that he had missed an opportune time to be one of them — by not having his sunglasses with him.

It was ruled that Haris would drive Javed's scooter, contingent on whether Javed could sit up straight on the scooter behind him. Haris had ascertained from various snippets of information that they all needed to hydrate for the next 48 hrs. Javed did not think he could ride on the back of the scooter. So Anjum and him decided to hail a rickshaw. Rashid felt alright to drive his own motorbike.

'But where are we going?' said Haris, unwilling to let them all part ways after the experience of the night.

'*Oh bhaiya me to jahanum jaa raha hoon tu aa ya na aa*. Brother I'm going to my own private hell right now whether you come or not!' Javed groaned.

'Let's go to the beach *yaar*!' Rashid suggested, the hazel in his eyes picking up the early light of the sun. Anjum looked askance. 'What about bed? Sweet bed?' he said.

'What??' said Rashid, 'Javed's already had a nap!'

'Yeah and he's also vomiting like an asshole!'

'No, no I'm better now — really,' suddenly the idea of the beach seemed like the perfect antidote to him. He thought of his hot, hot room — of the electricity playing it's cruel tricks on him and knew he did not want to be there.

His body felt like it had released a million demons — and he felt loose, free — albeit tinged with a touch of quease.

The ocean sounded like the right kind of tonic.

* * * * * *

It was 5 a.m. and the sands of Clifton Beach were glistening titanium in the crepuscular light. There was a purity to the air that could only be experienced at this time before the smog and pollution of the day took over. The only beings out were the stray dogs of Karachi that claimed the streets every night — ferociously chasing cars off, barking and biting at bumpers.

The rickshaw driver gave them a suspicious look after delivering them to their destination and then drove off rapidly, lurching a little. Rashid hopped off his motorbike, stretched his arms over his head and let out a whoop. 'This is the life brothers. This is the life!' They made their way shakily down to the sands. Haris began removing his garments down to his underwear.

'What the hell are you doing *yaara*?' asked Anjum unsure of Haris's strip-down.

'What? I'm like the fishermen bathing in the sea at sunrise!'

'Seems like the best idea I've ever heard,' said Javed, with a little less verve and abandon than Haris — also attempting to undress.

Anjum lay down on the sand and said he would join them later. Rashid, Haris and Javed made off to the restorative waters of Clifton Beach hoping not to step on any blue bottles, dog shit or rip their feet open on the shards of glass, or errant clips of barbed wire.

* * * * * *

When Javed woke at 8 p.m. to utter darkness in his room, he was disoriented. He did not know what time it was, what day it was — and for a while he did not even know where in the hell he was. Gradually, all the pieces came back together like an image coming into focus on a slide projector — and then flooded in. What Javed could *not* fathom was why he felt so utterly wretched.

It was the worst he had ever felt — like death, destruction and doom all had hung their coats on his coat-rack. He was hot and sticky, and there was no mistaking the feeling in his head for anything other than brutal pain.

He had no idea what to do — so he lay back down and watched the blades of his fan going round and round. How could he feel so low after feeling so much joy? He wanted to cry. He felt this great sense of loss — he felt desperate and confused and wanted to go back to that happy place where he was part of everything and everything was part of him.

He too was a golden child last night, and women — so many shining, polished women — had looked at him differently, not the way they did when he saw them in the streets of Clifton or Defence, as if he was a leper.

He had seen these same women free and open! As he drifted in and out of his thoughts, flashbacks and emotions — for no reason his mind rested on a memory of Zainab in yellow. A month or so had passed since his encounter with her at the Sunday market. Once in a while when he drove through Zamzama, and saw a well-groomed member of the female species walking as if on eggshells presumably due to a fresh pedicure — he wondered if it was her handiwork.

It was 9 p.m. and a train shrieked by outside — Javed clutching his head — watched blearily as his tiny Seiko clock bounced up and down on the table next to his bed. Sunday was over, and he couldn't bear the thought of going to work tomorrow. He felt about for his phone and called Anjum.

'Eh,' he grunted.

'Eh,' said Anjum equally huskily as if he hadn't actually used his mouth to talk to anyone in months.

'*Tu kesa hain*? How are you feeling?' Javed asked him.

'Not as good as one may expect,' Anjum said flatly.

'Yeah me too,' Javed agreed. Anjum relayed that Haris had been told that this may happen, so not to worry.

'Not to worry? I feel like putting a gun to my head and blowing my brains out! But luckily I have absolutely no energy to either find a gun or if I had one to lift one!' Anjum guffawed.

'Well at least you're making jokes.'

'Yeah,' Javed agreed, 'but I really don't want to go to work tomorrow *yaar*. Forget about wanting, I don't think I can!'

Anjum agreed totally, but luckily as a cameraman his schedule was not always 9-5 pm.

'What do you think I should do?' Javed asked Anjum.

'Well you don't ever take off from work man. Just take off! And for the rest of the night eat — drink, chill.'

'I'll call you tomorrow,' said Anjum. '*Chaal theek hain yaar*. Okay — sounds like a plan,' said Javed, who hung up and found himself crashing hard into a deep, deep sleep.

II
Raga Megh Malhar

1

Side-Winding

When you're poor in Karachi as in any urban centre, you cannot spend much time in your home, for the simple reason that it isn't comfortable enough. The rich can spend as much time as they like in their homes, for everything is present — food, service, conditioned air, hot water, cold water, drinking water — check, check, check — all of the above. Javed was out on his scooter driving around not so much aimlessly as without a specific destination. He was in Defence Phase 5, and that's all he knew.

He drove with leisure down Khyban-E-Badban — examining attentively *every* house on the street — he took pleasure in their shapes, sizes and forms. Each one appeared an elegant island within itself, individual kingdoms of beauty and art — fortified against the elements. Some chose to embed wicked shards of broken bottles in green, blue and brown into the wet cement of their outer walls to deter would-be intruders. Anyone who dared scale the wall would find themselves ripped to shreds and bleeding profusely. Others, chose barbed wire, in addition, for their defense systems. Gothic spikes too tipped with arrowheads adorned the peripheries of some walls. Armed guards stood watch.

He found himself fascinated by the gates of each house — often majestic, sometimes menacing but always acting as portals. Some were solid, mechanical sliding deals that clanked shut with a heavy bang. These gates barely allowed a peek at their precious containment.

Other houses had palatial wrought iron gates. If the stars aligned, Javed was privy to a good view of the cars, the garden and if he was very lucky, a peep of the interior of the house — *if* the front door opened at *just* the right angle.

He was alarmed at how many cars the majority of these mansions had parked inside. He mentally calculated how many people must live in there to warrant having six cars. Or were there just two inhabitants who just enjoyed using different cars? Maybe a few cars were for special occasions, others for everyday usage?

This was Javed's favourite pastime, that he *never* shared with anyone. Driving around and looking, basically *spying* on wealthy people's houses, counting their cars — the number of *chowkidaars*/watchmen and servants outside and above all the number of air conditioner vents sticking out of the walls of their houses — would most likely seem odd to his friends. There was a house near Bilawal House — the assassinated ex-prime minister Benazir Bhutto's family residence, that he always drove by on his frequent evening reccys.

It was located on a deserted corner. Its outer walls were constructed like a rock garden, with reams of magenta bougainvillea cascading forth. From the outside you could see a large sprawling balcony where people would sit, having snacks in the evening, drinking Rooh Afza, but the true *piece de resistance* was the gate. There was no other gate like it that Javed had seen on his travels around the elite areas of Karachi. It was about 30 ft high, as imposing as a Mughal palace gate and was constructed of panels of thick, impenetrable wood with iron slats running around each panel. For ornament there were intricately designed iron studs in the centre of every panel, and at the top of the gate wooden turrets.

His favourite bit was a small window in the gate that sometimes opened if a car was waiting outside. It was the gatekeeper's window, and a face would peer through, discerning who sought entry to the palace. The house was shrouded with greenery, making visibility difficult but from the wall that Javed could see over from the main road, he had counted three air conditioner vents to two windows.

Once, he had been counting vertically the array of air conditioner vents on a massive apartment block and noticed that only one window did not have a vent installed in it. He felt sorry for the people living there, the odd ones out. They had managed to procure a fancy apartment but could not get the air conditioner to go with the lifestyle. He wondered about their circumstances. A few months later, he had driven by the same apartment block and felt sorry no more — that same apartment had the largest, newest looking air conditioner in the whole block, and it was a split level, it was above the window and capable of cooling three rooms.

The most impressive house in the whole city to his mind was the house on the hill in *Gizri* opposite the graveyard. This house defied all his attempts at voyeurism, for it was situated too high up to peep at, and the walls were too high on the street on which it sat. It was rumoured to be owned by an Arab sheikh. When you drove up the hill towards *Gizri* it watched you imperiously its many lights twinkling and luxuriating glamour; however, its multiple balconies, always empty, looked unused and lonely.

When he wound up the hill and drove past it, the outer walls went on for an eternity. There were multiple gates. Sometimes, these gates would open and he would spy long, winding driveways and split-level construction.

He could never actually park his scooter and observe, unless he pretended to have stopped to fix something and even then he would get shooed off by the loyal watchmen serving their masters and mistresses. If he stood too long, they would threaten to call the police, which for a man like him with no power, and no connections would be the end of his life. Nobody knew what really went on in Pakistani jails, but one thing was clear: if you were ill-connected or simply poor, one wrong move and you were at their mercy. If you were wealthy and well-connected chances are you would never once have a single conversation with a policeman or see the inside of a jail cell even if you went on a killing spree with a machine gun. As long as you were rich enough to own the latest Chloe handbag and drove a Pajero — chances are nobody could touch you, ever.

Seaview was the most puzzling to Javed. They were the premium beach-front apartments that people had been dying to own for decades. There had been waiting-lists longer than the span of the Arabian ocean along the Karachi coast, but the lack of understanding about beach-front construction had very quickly turned them into buildings that looked dessicated. Those who had coveted the beach-front life soon discovered that Clifton Beach was no prize and the price of living in front of the Arabian Ocean was a rapid disintegration of all their possessions.

There was no question of opening one's windows to enjoy the cool ocean air, for that air was full of humidity that killed all electronics within a short span of time. Yet Javed heard how much these apartments went for. As he drove around the tangled labyrinth that was the Seaview complex, with roads full of potholes and saw the rust on all the windows, the peeling paint, the rotting walls he decided that he very definitely did not want to live there. Every few blocks, there would be one apartment that had attempted to make the best of a bad deal by re-doing the exterior. A few months on, and the sea breeze — the great reducer would have levelled out all their hard work and made their flat look again the same as those of everybody else. Like a curse.

No, there was nowhere Javed wanted to live more than in the house on the hill — closer to the sky, lording it over the whole city. This was one of two hills in an otherwise flat Karachi, and the more desirable. The house was placed smack-bang in the centre. Nobody commanded such a view and many a night Javed would imagine what it looked like inside — and the lives of those who lived there.

* 2 *

Something Like Timbuktu

Since Javed's pharmaceutical adventure, he had been feeling different. When he was loafing around Ami *paan* shop — in Defence, or at Boat Basin in Clifton — he felt more at home, and could have sworn that people, and in particular, women were being nicer to him. It was as if they knew, they all knew and Javed had inadvertently been initiated into the secret cult of status. Javed and his friends had discovered that 'Ee', as Haris called it, elongating the breath, was extremely dangerous if one did not drink water constantly. 'Ee' caused over-heating and, yes, vomiting — so everything Javed had endured had been a result of improper usage.

'I could have died, you asshole!' he had yelled at Haris, not *as* mad at him as he was making out. Perhaps sometimes one had to risk everything, even life itself, in order to transcend one's own reality.

Regardless, it was mutually agreed that the night *had* been a rollicking success. They now knew what all the fuss was about. Rashid was eager for another hit. Anjum rolled his eyes.

'Dude it was a miracle, yeah? And believe me miracles are like lightning they don't strike twice. *Bhool jao yeh sub kuch*. Forget all this now.' Javed wasn't sure that he could handle another night of that intensity. The way he had plummeted into the Slough of Despondency had been unnerving.

Upon some investigation it was discovered that the drug dealers would cut the pills with other drugs, such as heroin, ketamine and cocaine, all of which ensured you would come down, down, down after you soared up. Rashid, unsurprisingly, had been unaffected by the doldrums. He had a natural bouyancy, and seemed to go through life totally unfettered by the kind of anxieties and desires that the rest of the world endured.

Javed envied him in this. His own desire to transcend his circumstances, bordering on obsession, and his dissatisfaction with his status in life sometimes felt unbearable. A part of him wished he could abandon his desires and be a happier man like his friend, but then again, he wondered if perhaps he, Javed, actually knew exactly what he needed to be happy and Rashid did not.

It was a Wednesday evening, midweek. The sun had finally gone to bed, freeing the denizens of Karachi from her ruthless hold. Javed had come straight to Sher Jaan's tea house after work starving, and in need of refreshment. He had not told Sher Jaan about his eventful 'Ee' night, for he knew the man would not understand and disapprove on principle. He sat there drinking tea whilst listening to the ocean roar. Perhaps he would be better off like Sher Jaan, sitting here by the ocean every night, making *naans*, friends coming and going — this wasn't a bad life. It was just after 8 p.m. and Javed was about ready to make the journey home after a long day, when he heard a female voice.

'*Asalam-a-Laikum*!'

'*Va Laikum Bibi ji*! And *salaam* back to you, miss!' he heard Sher Jaan reply. It couldn't be, Javed thought. How? Why? He got off the *charpai* that was his spot behind the *naan* shop and headed inside towards the front entrance where he saw her.

'Zainab Miss... Miss Zainab... Zainab?' he managed to utter flustered, trying to curtail a smile that wanted to flood his face. '*Asalam-a Laikum*!'

It was Zainab, demure but confident — just as when he had met her.

'Please *ai ai bethey*! Please come in and sit down,' Javed began to fuss over her formally, as if the place was his, whilst Sher Jaan too fussed over her — there was a lot of fussing in the *dhaba*.

Women were not a feature here. Especially not unaccompanied women, who were so young and beautiful. Everyone was flummoxed. If it had been anywhere else — the men would have stared and stared at her openly, as was the national pastime amongst the men in Pakistan, but here amongst Sher Jaan's crew there was no such disrespect.

Zainab looked around and chose to sit at a table in the outside seating area. '*Aap idhr*? You here?' Javed had to ask. 'Well, you had said that you spent a lot of time here in the evenings and that Sher Jaan *chacha* made the best *Aloo chola* and tea in Karachi so I thought I'd come and see for myself!'

'*Magar akalay*? But alone?' Javed could not resist the temptation to air his concern.

'*Ji*, Javed saab. Yes, Mr. Javed,' Zainab replied nonplussed, '*Akalay*! You did say Sher Jaan was like a father to you, so I figured if you trusted him than I trusted him too!'

Javed peered intently into his teacup still curbing the free dispersal of his smiles. There was no arguing with her. And she was right — whether he had been here or not — she would have been safe at Sher Jaan's.

'Okay, but what about getting back home in the dark... and so late?' Javed asked.

'My dear Javed,' Zainab replied, 'I have a cell phone

and I have the number of a taxi company that I use often if it gets late. What difference does it make if they pick me up from work, or from the beach or *Choo Choo Ki Maleyaan*!' At the mention of the comical, imaginary destination that meant something like Timbuktu, Javed allowed the laughter to overshadow his concern.

'*Phir bhi Zainab ji. Even so Zainab-ji*,' Javed added softly, '*Aap ladies ko ahteyaat karna chaheeye*! You ladies need to be careful.'

Sher Jaan came over to the table with a cup of hot tea for Zainab. Placing it in front of her, he exclaimed '*Aap ka bauhat shukriya Bibi ke aap humare dhabey pur iss raat aiyye*! I thank you miss that you have come to our humble teashop!' Zainab told him of Javed's advance publicity that had lured her here.

'Yes Javed iss gud bwoy.' he boomed thumping him on the back.

Then Sher Jaan too launched into a health and safety interrogation. Zainab could not argue with him and instead just nodded silently punctuating the movement with '*Ji, ji.* Yes, yes of course,' every few seconds. Sher Jaan eventually left having extracted a promise from her that if she ever came alone again she would have the rickshaw or taxi park right next to the tea shop and when she left, he personally would oversee the driver — as the whole stretch of beach was full of taxi and rickshaw drivers who were his friends and would never, ever disrespect him.

'Yes Sher Jaan *ji*. No Sher Jaan *ji*,' Zainab said obediently.

Javed grinned at her and wagged his finger whilst Sher Jaan wasn't looking.

'*Allah*!' Zainab sighed in mock-weariness when Sher Jaan finally made his way back to this tandoori oven, 'Well, that's what you get!' Javed said.

'Anyway, can we talk about something else now? *Mera police interrogation aab mukamal ho giya*? Is my police interrogation complete?'

'Not quite,' said Javed, '*Aap kesee hain*? *Aur aap itnee der se kyo niklee hain*? How are you? And seriously, how is it you came out so late? Everything alright?'

Zainab did not want to reveal to Javed that her wastrel brother had come close to physical violence with her and her mother the night before, and that she didn't want to go home.

It was also true, however, that before the incident she had been feeling restless all week, 'The women who come to my salon are always going somewhere! You know? Some women come every single day to get their hair and make-up done. Every day! There is a *shaadi*, there is a tea party — there is a dinner party,' said Zainab.

Javed nodded silently sensing the over-wrought emotion in her. 'The thought of going home after I left the salon today...' she veered off, '... the electricity has been gone everyday when I've reached home and I just didn't want to sit in the heat and dark in my house today hearing my mother yelling at my brothers, you know?' she looked down, embarrassed.

Javed too felt embarrassed just on principle, but said, 'Don't worry. It's good you came here. And I am glad that I was here too.'

'Yes,' Zainab shook her head, 'I was hoping to see you,' she said with what seemed like studied nonchalance.

The words did cause Javed's heart to jump in an unexpected manner.

He made sure she ate up and they talked about the last month — although Javed was careful not to mention his 'Ee' night. A woman like Zainab would probably not think too much of his and his friends shenanigans, and he felt no need to boast or squawk.

There was a silent comfort in Zainab's company, one that he had not experienced in any woman's company. He felt neither awkward, nor did he feel like he needed to puff out his chest and beat it the way he had seen his friends do on the rare occasion that a member of the female species had been around. They talked of Karachi, of Zainab's family, of what her no-good brothers had been up to or not up to, as it were — with Zainab careful not to divulge the bulk of the pain and suffering she endured at their hands.

In Javed's company, she felt that same safety — that same care that she remembered from their first meeting. Javed, oblivious to what she was thinking, told her about his roots in North Nazimabad, about his work at the ID card office.

The night had turned into a cool dream. Javed felt not one iota of the heat of the day on him. It was nearing 10 o'clock, and he was concerned about Zainab's homeward journey.

'I want to walk on the beach,' Zainab said.

'But... but ...' Javed mumbled aware of the connotations to the rest of the world of an unmarried man and women walking in the dark on the beach, besides which if the police saw them there might be trouble.

Zainab said, 'Please Javed don't worry I am happy to

go on my own.' That was a completely unacceptable option to Javed. No, no, he must accompany her and to hell with it. If the police found her alone — it may be much, much worse.

'I haven't walked here in many, many years,' Zainab said softly as the sound of the ocean roared in their ears. The smell of salt tinged with dead fish carried on the air.

'Well you can tell me any time you want to,' said Javed graciously, 'and I will accompany you.'

'Thank you Javed,' said Zainab. They walked on in silence for a while. The camel riders of the beach, their bells and decorations jangling after a long day of being paid to take children for rides betwixt the humps of their camels, trudged slowly past them.

'Do you remember the ship?' Zainab asked out of the blue.

'Do I?' Javed said, 'Of course!'

'Do you know where it came from?' she asked hopefully.

'No! Do you?'

'No,' Zainab replied, 'I suppose it's just one of life's inexplicable mysteries,' and Javed nodded silently in agreement.

* * * * * *

He had not wanted to make her uncomfortable, but he had a vehicle and saw no reason why she should spend good money going home when he could take her. The only obvious hurdle was the proximity at which they would have to sit, and she would have to hold him.

He really wanted to see her home safely, but feeling practically paralyzed, he could not ask her in case she saw it as an affront. The voices in his head that he was having an internal debate with therefore decided against it. It would have been disrespectful.

He decided instead that he was going to hail a rickshaw for her with a driver he knew well and follow her home anyway, but then would she think he was trying to find out where she lived? There was just no way to win in this situation he realized, and so made the offer hoping for the best.

Zainab brushed it off with a quick retort. That was ridiculous. Why should he go out of his way like that? She was having none of it, and enough was enough of the protectiveness. She was going to go with a safe, secure taxi company and pay the extra money to make sure.

It was then that Javed realized he had no way of contacting Zainab once she left. His heart sank. What if this was it? Why would Zainab want to see him again anyway? Well perhaps she needed some help again, after all she had found him this time. As they waited for the taxi he got more and more anxious that he would never see Zainab again but could not open his mouth to utter any words. The white cab drew up.

She had not been able to stop Sher Jaan, Javed and Sher Jaan's brother, all from waiting with her for the taxi and having a few words with the taxi driver before she got in. The young wiry lad looked nonplussed. He was used to this, it happened all the time. The mobilization of women in Pakistan was a new thing, and the men almost always felt insecure about letting them go off on their own, and were wont to have a word with the taxi drivers before sending off their cargo.

Zainab sat in the cab, and rolled down the window, '*Khuda Hafiz*! Goodbye!' she waved joyfully.

'Next Wednesday? Same place?' she asked. Javed experienced an overwhelming feeling of relief as his innards were released from the tight knot they had been in, and replied simply, 'As you wish,' with a flourish and Zainab was gone.

Sher Jaan patted him on the back with a resounding thump, saying, '*Mashallah mashallah*. Very gud. Very gud gurrl,' mixing in English again uncharacteristically as if the occasion warranted such pomp — whilst Javed stared out at the sea, unwilling to utter a word lest he jinx the moment in some way.

* 3 *

Pakistan Zindabad

The monsoon season was coming to Karachi. Every year, during the monsoons it rained incessantly — the type of heavy, tropical rain that could bring real joy to farmers and those afflicted by the heat. In Karachi it started a reign of chaos. The roads very soon gave way, and within weeks giant potholes would appear or the rain would collect in the potholes that already existed; either way Karachi was rendered untraversable. And this happened *every* year.

The first heavy rains began at sometime in the wee hours at the end of July — by the time commuter traffic started it was still in full swing. Four feet of rain had fallen in 7 hours, and by 10 a.m. the roundabout at the Two Swords had cars marooned around it practically floating helplessly.

Motorcyclists were up on the kerb having heaved their vehicles up and sat chatting as if on their own private island in the centre of Karachi. That was the thing about Pakistan — people did not get overly distraught about catastrophe. How could they when, whether man-made or natural, they were subjected to it on a regular basis. So they couldn't get into work. It was okay. Nobody else could either and nobody expected any different.

As the week went on, the news was filled with stories of billboards out on various roads having fallen down under the duress of the rains and winds, and a general alert was put out to everybody to try not to be near them or electrical poles during the rain, or after the rain. This, however was never a deterrent to anybody in Karachi. As Javed attempted to make his way to work, trousers rolled up to his knees every day, he marvelled at the capacity of nature to turn the lives of man upside down. The road outside Ideal Bakery had stayed flooded about 3 feet high all week, the land was turning to ocean; there seemed to be not much difference between the two.

It became a common sight to see bands of men helping one another push their cars out of a deep water pocket. Their clothes would be soaked, but they would be laughing and pushing at the same time. Javed himself had twice stopped to assist — once an elderly professor at Karachi University and a second time a driver taking his Begum to Agha's supermarket.

There was never any question of a person attempting to get out of a sticky spot alone. If you were in trouble on the road, at any time of the year — let alone in the monsoons in Karachi, you could guarantee that not just one or two but a whole group of people would magically appear to assist you.

Javed sat on the window ledge of his room smoking a Gold Leaf in his hostel after five hours on the road in total to and from work, when usually it was one hour each way. Despite being exhausted, he felt strangely peaceful. The monsoons were the great levellers — and there was always a certain modicum of excitement to the chaos that they brought. The air was deliciously cool as he sat in his Mercury vest and loose shalwar.

It was Wednesday, and he had risked life and limb to get to Sher Jaan's that evening — but Zainab had never come. It was unlikely that she would; how could she have? Rickshaws had a bad time of it in the season of deluge, and certainly she couldn't afford the snazzy taxi service, with clean, new cars every time... the beat-up old black and yellow taxis fared worse than the rickshaws... both vehicles that seemed held together by sheer force of will the rest of the year, gave up the ghost in the monsoons.

Perhaps he would never see her again. One never knew what could happen to people during the monsoons. Once they were finally over you would hear stories of people dispossessed, killed in an electrical pole mishap, or drowned caught in the current in the Arabian Ocean. He realized he was being overly morbid, shook it off and went to get a cup of tea from the communal kitchen of the hostel.

* * * * * *

August 14th, Independence Day — arrived smack dab in the middle of the wet season. Every year the armed forces had a special event that was televised all over the country. People clustered around their television sets to see the air display, the marching and the shooting. Flags usually started appearing a few weeks before. Some, made of cloth usually the large ones would appear in the markets for sale, others made of paper constructed into banners of hundreds of different-coloured flags would adorn the outsides of houses and shops. Javed loved this time of the year. Everyone on the streets seemed full of good-will and comraderie.

He and his friends met in the morning to eat hot *halwa poori* and fragrant *cholaas* and then go on a drive waving flags and yelling 'Pakistan *Zindabad*! Long Live Pakistan,' like all the other male motorcycles crews did on August 14th.

Suzuki vans with people hanging out the back and off the sides drove shrieking and yelling joyfully by. Luckily, the rain had temporarily abated for a few days in advance so some roads had recovered, allowing more freedom of movement. Others however, had just become pools of stagnant water trapping anyone who attempted to drive through them.

They drove down the Ideal Bakery road in an attempt

to get to Seaview but found themselves adrift with other marooned souls. People had altogether abandoned the enterprise and were sitting idly on the strip of grass embedded in concrete that divided the two-way traffic. Some wore Pakistan flag pins, some waved flags. The air of revellry and celebration was palpable. A little further up some guys were making joints in the middle of the road, in the middle of the day — in the midst of the chaos of the monsoon floods.

Javed and his friends decided to join them. As Javed sat stoned in the middle of Clifton, watching the traffic trying to get by, he noticed a curious thing: none of the expensive cars carrying their dear cargo of elite Karachi were sporting any emblems of patriotism. The expressions of the people in the cars were sour and dissatisfied. It was the drivers of these cars who, finding themselves stuck in a pothole, yelled and fulminated at people trying to help them, whilst their employers sat put in their Honda Civics staring out of the window, as random passers-by tried to haul their seated fat asses along the road. Javed started giggling at that. Anjum looked over at him.

'*Kiya hoa?* Whattup?'

'*Buss yaar ye nazaara-e- aam*! Oh nothing just this spectacle of people.'

'Yeah it's a total fish market!' Anjum agreed, laughing.

They seemed to have sat there for hours. Getting steadily more red-eyed — they started singing songs. Soon, some other guys too started singing vociferously

'*Pakistan ka mutlab kiya! La Illaha Ilallah*! What is the meaning of Pakistan? There is no God but Allah!' This was the cue for Javed and his friends to move on. They were Allah-loving Muslims like the next man. But these days this type of out-and-out religiosity was something they steered clear of. You never knew where the next fundoo was going to spring from with a bomb strapped to his person.

They managed to continue their travels towards their sacred place in the madness of Karachi — the beach. At one point Haris's motorbike got too much water in its exhaust. It started choking and sputtering, so they waited for it to dry off at a *khoka* by the side of the road — siting on rickety chairs drinking Thumbs Up and smoking cigarettes. The proprietor of the *khoka* was an elderly man who they referred to simply as *Chacha*.

'Have you guys noticed,' started Javed, 'how today it is the poorest people who are out on the streets celebrating? How it's us who are most excited?'

'*Kiya bakwaas kar raha hain Mr Philosopher?* What are you on about Mr Philosopher?' replied Anjum, lightly.

'Well just look around. All the big cars have no flags, there are definitely no Begums hanging out the windows yelling Pakistan Zindabad!' The image which made them laugh.

'Yeah, I guess you're right,' agreed Anjum, '*Yeh hi to haal hain yaar*. This is the state of things friend.'

'You're right! Overhearing people in the markets, or at work... it's always the guy with the biggest house, the largest car or the aunty with the most gold dripping off her who will start complaining about '*yeh mulk...* '*yeh mulk,*' *to barbaad ho giya.* this country, this country. This country is destroyed... this'n'that. These people are crazy!' Javed exclaimed passionately.

'Those who have the biggest problems because of the inefficiency of the country... electricity, water etc... they have the most passion in their hearts for the country,' Rashid precised and Haris in a falsetto voice mimicking or mocking a 'Begum' said, 'Oh my Gott! I am so sick and tired of filling petrol in my generator — I tell you darrrrling,' an uproar of laughter followed.

'I think,' said Javed, starting to stand up on his chair unsteadily under the effect of the multiple joints they had smoked, 'there should be a law! The more air conditioners and generators you have the less right you have to complain!' They laughed.

'Yah! And sunglasses! And Pajeros! And mobile phones!' Chimed in Rashid, Haris and Anjum aping a trendy talking fashionably into his fashionable phone running his fingers through his hair, shoulders and chest all puffed out. They all lifted their bottles of Thumbs Up, cheering in unison, 'Pakistan Zindabad!'

* 4 *

Island Of Fools

The worst part about the monsoons was that — whereas the rest of the year load-shedding occurred on an albeit shaky semblance of a schedule — once the rains commenced, the Karachi Electrical Board had absolutely no reason to adhere to it anymore. Now they had a justifiable excuse — and so, the electricity went on a schedule of whenever, for inordinate amounts of time, due to various malfunctions, such as the fizzling out and scorching of cables, wires and poles all over the city; water trumping fire.

Initially, the rain had brought a kind of excitement with it for Javed — by about a month and a half of it, his patience and that of all Karachi dwellers started to wear very, very thin. Everywhere you went people would be complaining about endless phone calls to KEB which had resulted in nothing, or abrupt hang-ups or the line being busy for hours. The worst stories were of people queuing for days outside the KEB offices or those whose electricity just vanished one night and never came back. These stories were all you heard.

Javed did not live in an affluent area and his hostel was hit quite badly by the effects of the rains. The roads under Clifton Bridge were some of the worst. The whole area near the Cantt Train Station was like the land that time forgot. Twice already there had been a loud boom, when the lights went out and would not return till the next evening. Life was becoming increasingly impossible.

He spent his evenings reading his books of poetry by Faiz, Allama Iqbal and Mir Taqi Mir by candlelight. Getting anywhere but to work and back had become a nightmare, even telephonic communication was affected as the rains just came down like a great dam in the sky had burst. The trains outside his hostel continued unabated, ripping through the silence of the night made more poignant by the absence of the hum of electricity. He felt no peace, and grew increasingly restless — day by day.

On the day that the cyclone warning came, Javed was at the end of his tether. He had made his way to work after being stuck in the roads for hours and hours, only to get there and find out that people were being warned to stay away from the sea and move as far inland as possible.

Considering the city of Karachi was smack bang on the coast it was a rather difficult proposition. They shut the National ID card offices down early to allow people to get to shelter. Javed felt like he just didn't care anymore. He hadn't shaved in a few days and was looking a little rough. All those sleepless nights were catching up with him. Zainab had started to seem like a distant memory.

Driving away from work, he was surprised to find himself driving straight towards the sea rather than away from it. He had wanted to check on Sher Jaan anyway. It had been too long since he had seen him. And if the cyclone did hit, he would go down with the ship, i.e. the tea shop. Where would he go inland anyway? As he was pulling up to the eerily deserted Clifton beach, Anjum rang.

'Where are you?'

'I'm at the beach,' Javed said calmly.

'Have you lost your mind?'

'No,' said Javed.

'I think you have,' disagreed Anjum.

'Look man, I spent three hours getting to work and I'd rather be sitting right here than get back on my motorcycle and sit in traffic for another three hours. If the cyclone hits I'd rather die here than in my hole of a room!' Javed's voice grew progressively louder — surprising even himself.

There was a contemplative pause on the other end of the line before Anjum said sombrely, 'What you're saying makes sense. I'm in the same boat. I think I'll come too. Let me call Haris and Rashid.'

Haris and Rashid were feeling equally reckless that evening, which is how the four of them came to be found sitting on the wall of Clifton Beach watching the sky turn green and grey on the evening of the cyclone warning. Their families had rung to make sure their sons were safely sequestered away. Nobody dared tell their worried parents, siblings, grandparents, aunts and uncles exactly where they were. It felt good. None of them felt they had a deathwish. They simply wanted to wait and see what would happen.

The sky rumbled and shifted like a woman's stomach in which a baby was moving around. There was something ominous about the evil green colour, and the persistent strikes of lightning that sprang directly downwards in vertical lines like the grinning teeth of a shining skull.

'The cyclone is coming man. Look at the sky! It looks angry!' said Haris, finally. Rashid turned to him squinting against the strong winds trying to blow the gritty sand into his eyes. His hair was flying in all directions, his white shirt billowing out like the sail of a ship. 'You do realize that if the cyclone does come it will be so fast that we will not have any time to run for cover,' he yelled over the wind, the voice of the pragmatist on the island of fools.

A jangling sound filled their ears and the camel riders

came galloping by. The reds, greens, magentas and yellows of their regalia blurred into bright streaks against the backdrop of the sand and sea. They were rushing urgently to some semblance of safety, but where could camels hide in a cyclone Javed wondered? A familiar Nokia tune began ringing on the airwaves. It was Javed's phone. He stared at his phone for a second frowning as he could not recognize the number. They all turned to look at him. Javed punched the green button and lifted the phone to his ear. Soon he was nodding and frowning.

'What about your family?'

'You really think so?'

'I can just take you home,' they heard him saying.

Haris shot Anjum a quizzical look who in turn shot Rashid a quizzical look. Javed hung up the phone and all at once, the thunderous look on his face dissipated after what seemed like an age. It had been Zainab. She was stuck near her salon and could not get a ride anywhere. He had told her he and his friends were in fact at the beach, and without missing a beat she had said she wanted to join them. Javed had tried to dissuade her saying it wasn't safe and so on and so forth — but Zainab made the good point that if it was so unsafe why was he risking all to sit there.

He tried to convince her that she should be with her family if the cyclone did hit. She said she would never get home by the time they were saying the cyclone would hit, so she might as well not bother. Javed knew he wanted to see her more than anything, despite the rather dramatic circumstances. His friends looked at him for an explanation.

Javed: 'I have to go and pick up Zainab'.

All three voices: 'Who's Zainab?'

'I'm not really sure how to explain and I don't have time.'

Haris, Anjum and Rashid did not bother to ask anymore questions.

'You guys wait here. She isn't far.'

'But what if something happens while you're gone *yaar*?' Anjum asked very seriously.

'If something happens...' Javed looked out at the sea feeling reassured by the joy he was feeling, 'Nothing's going to happen.' They nodded silently in unison.

* * * * * *

It turned out that getting to Zainab and back was a great deal easier than he had imagined, for the roads were deserted. She was sitting on the concrete steps outside a fancy boutique, with the cuffs of her *shalwar* rolled up slightly holding her *chappals* in one hand. The mannequins in the window stood peering out of their window with heavy black wrought iron security gates over them, looking for all the world like they wanted to escape.

He parked on the opposite side of the street from her, as her side was flooded.

'Zainab!' She looked up and with a big smile waved at him.

'Can you get over to this side?' he yelled. She looked up and down the road, and nodded. There was a small dry patch a little further down. Javed watched her manoeuvre gracefully and with confidence. She did not seem distressed in the least bit that the destruction of her city, her family, and her life could be imminent. Or perhaps she, too, like most Karachi-ites and Pakistanis had become immune to chaos and catastrophe.

Zainab was dressed in a deep emerald *kameez shalwar* that seemed to be embossed with a design like green fire. Her dupatta was half on her head, half off and the bottom of it was wet. Her dark hair fell over her face. It was wet and rather bedraggled. '*Aslam-a-laikum*,' she said as she approached him. 'Thank you a million times over Javed.'

Javed did not say a word. He was dumbfounded by the beauty of Zainab against the backdrop of this deserted and dangerous city. He felt like he was going to vomit at the prospect of her sitting behind him on the motorbike.

'Have you sat on a motor bike before?' he asked. She had, her brother had one once. Yes, she knew how to sit. She looked up at the sky as it rumbled and for a moment looked concerned. 'Are your friends really sitting there waiting for you on the sea wall?' she asked. Javed nodded and said softly, 'But Zainab I can still take you home. In fact, let me do that.' She looked at him seriously for a moment and then laughed her deep laugh, 'Are you joking! And miss the action?' The last thing she wanted to do was go home.

As always, Javed was surprised by this woman. He smiled a little half-heartedly wishing he had not come to get her — feeling gravely concerned about taking her into the jaws of death so to speak, second-guessing his decision to tell her where he had been when she had called. She probably would have been safer here if the cyclone did hit.

Zainab looked at him straight in the eyes and said, 'Javed you know this isn't your fault'. 'What do you mean?' he asked.

'I was calling you to ask you if you wanted to go to the beach,' she said still looking directly at him. For the very first time he looked at Zainab straight on and locked eyes for a split-second, in which the entire universe seemed to turn on its head, and he understood. He needed to shake off this deeply-rooted patriarchy.

This woman had a mind of her own and by some bizarre co-incidence her mind and his were linked. What were the odds?

* * * * * *

Along the coast of Karachi are seven shrines. The myth goes that because these shrines stand guard at the seafront, the storms always narrowly miss the city. The cyclone never came, not even the rain came that evening. There was just a series of dissatisfied rumblings of the *jinns* of the sky angered at being prevented from letting loose. By 9 p.m. the storm warning had pretty much been called off as the meteorologists watched the cloud that was worrying them trundle off to wreak its havoc on some other coast or in the middle of the sea.

Seaview still remained deserted as were all the restaurants on the sea front, but by that time they were absolutely ravenous and made their way to Boat Basin to have burgers and *chaat*. They were confident that Boat Basin would never shut. Zainab had gotten along with his friends remarkably well, and the boys also seemed to take a shine to her. They were all astonished, there was no denying that — as they would tell him later, at her sudden appearance — and then not only at how beautiful she was but also calm, well-spoken and not giggly like so many of the women they came across.

'She didn't even have one scrap of make-up on her face *yaar*,' Rashid had remarked — so used to the plastered faces of Karachi women coming into his shop.

When Javed told them that she supported her whole family they were just as gob-smacked as he had been. 'Man, you must have done something right in your life that this angel from heaven came to you!' Anjum said. Javed brushed him off, after all Zainab was not his property or his... he felt himself blushing furiously, 'girlfriend'. She was just Zainab.

'It's not like that,' he explained.

'I merely help her when she needs help. That's all,' he explained somberly.

'I don't even have her phone number in my phone.'

'Well,' said Anjum in a rational manner, 'she obviously likes you or she wouldn't have called you when she thought the world was going to end, right?' and Javed decided that Anjum had in fact, made a very good point.

III

Raag Marwa

After The Monsoons

After the cyclone-scare, Javed saw Zainab more often — but still only when she called him. He went cell phone shopping with her, facilitating the best deal. He had buddies working in the phone shops, so Zainab was suitably impressed with his range of contacts. They spent more time at Sher Jaan's, and Javed often marvelled at the fact that there was never any awkwardness between them or talk of being 'girlfriend' and 'boyfriend'. He realized he had started feeling inexplicably lighter, as if a huge burden he never knew existed had been weighing on him and now was gone. His days and nights were spent easier.

It was a Thursday night, the night that worshippers visited the shrine of Abdullah Shah Ghazi amidst music and revellry. Zainab had expressed a desire to visit it sometime but had never been able to go, being an unaccompanied female. Javed promised that he would accompany her. He was to pick Zainab up from work at 6 so they could eat something and then make their way to the shrine.

She was late but managed to text him. She had been kept late at work but would hopefully be done by 7. If he wanted to leave she would understand. But Javed waited outside her salon patiently — watching at a deferential distance as women breezed out of the salon door in a cloud of perfume and hairspray — like beautiful androids put together in a factory, sharing the same glossy locks — their clothes flowing and immaculate.

He chuckled inwardly as a few women came out bare foot with some strange contraption lodged between their toes, with their maids carrying their shoes behind them ordering that their driver be called right up to the curb so they could get in their cars. The toenail polish must not be compromised.

Javed shook his head and continued to wait for Zainab. Finally she was freed. To Javed she looked like the only woman to come out of there who was real. She did not look happy though, so he treaded carefully.

'*Asalam a laikum* Javed,' she said formally as she always did.

'*Va Laikum Zainab ji,*' said Javed.

'*Kheriyat?* Are you alright?' Zainab said nothing was wrong — it had been a long day. Was she too tired? No. She would be fine after some food, and thank you for waiting but you really didn't have to.

They decided to go to get some kebab rolls at the hot spot nearby — Kebab Hotel. They sat on the flimsy tables outside amongst the throng of people eager for kebab rolls — cars honking, smoke rising, and worried-looking waiters running back and forth. Zainab looked off into the distance, a million miles away.

Once she started eating she perked up a little. 'Actually today was one of the worst days I've had in a long time,' she finally revealed. Javed was all ears, she so rarely told him about her work. 'There were just so many...' and she pulled a face wrinkling up her nose with an expression of dissatisfaction looking for the right words, '...*SARREYAL BEGUMS*! Sour Begums!' she said in a way that indicated relief at finally calling them that.

'*Oof! Yeh ghalat kar rahee ho. Vo ghalat kar rahee ho.* You are doing this wrong. You are doing that wrong.' Then

I got some dye on someone's clothes and... God forgive me for repeating this profanity... *You uloo ki pathi*! You owl's daughter! This suit cost 36,000 ruppees!' Mostly I have regular customers. But some days the regulars are nowhere to be seen and only new customers stream in, who can be very unpleasant.'

Javed was frowning, feeling more and more anger as he listened to Zainab. He couldn't bear the thought of these women treating her like this, talking to her like this. He bit at his lip furiously.

'It seems like tonight every house in Karachi is having a party,' Zainab said, not entirely without humour.

'I have been helping women get ready since the morning. Some women arrived at 12 o'clock and didn't leave till 6! Hair, nails, face... this'n'that...'

She did not feel it appropriate to talk about the hair removal practices of the women of Karachi's upper crust in front of a man so did not say more about it. However, she continued to nurse her bitter resentment towards the women who were one step away from pitching a tent in the beauty parlour, in order to have every single hair on their bodies (except perhaps their eyebrows and eyelashes) removed. Even the soft, almost unnoticeable down on their backs had to be remedied about twice a week. Sometimes Zainab had to send them away as there was no hair to remove.

There was one treatment that particularly bothered her. It was the skin-whitening treatment, and it was the most popular. Even her colleagues, a host of giggly and insecure girls were always giving each other these treatments. They were obsessed with being — as it was called '*gorri*' or white-r.

Every woman who came through the door was

commented upon, '*Hai kitnee kaali hain.* How dark/black she is,' with horror, or alternatively,'*Hai kitnee gorri hain.* How fair she is,' in admiration.

Those who were *kaali* and happily oblivious were immediately convinced in so many words while they were getting their manicure done that they should get the whitening facial. Even the women who were not *kaali*, but quite *gorri* got the treatment — ostensibly as a preventative measure against the darkening of their sacred fair skin and to assure their continued 'fairness'. The fairer the customer, the more Zainab's colleagues would fawn all over them, as if a code was embedded in their DNA programming; the degree of subservience to a person in direct proportion to the relative lightness of their skin.

Zainab herself was on the dark side of what was called '*sanwali*' or 'wheatish complexion' — considered an acceptable standard. Indeed, most of the women who came through her parlour were this colour. It was modifiable by the whitening treatment, and even without, it could be improved upon with make-up. Many, if not all of the girls who worked with her were quite dark in skin colour, and attempted assiduously to change that. Sometimes, she might snap at them if she heard the word '*gorri/white*' come out of their mouths one more time, other times she just couldn't be bothered.

On the rare occasion that she had time to flick through the Western magazines that lay stacked in the parlour she saw models that were dark as the night, black like the Makranis — dressed in Egyptian golds, bronzes, coppers with crimson that glowed on their lips and viridian that sparkled like verdant fields on their lids and thought how absolutely magnificent they looked. Her companions were always less than impressed by the black models, exclaiming in shock:

'*Hai! Uff Allah*! She's so black! How did they put her in a magazine?'

Instead of taking heart, and confidence, from darker women in Western magazines, and perhaps getting a message that it was okay to be dark, these girls in turn denigrated them and themselves in the process. There was no other colour to be but fair. And that was that. If your eyes were green or blue, the combination of which was found in the Indian actress Kareena Kapoor — then in the eyes of the majority of Pakistani women from any class you were the ideal of beauty: fair skinned and light eyed.

Zainab tried to work with colours that she believed suited darker skin more when she had time. On slow days the girls were able to experiment on each other, get some treatments, practice and play. She had decided that in order for darker girls to look their most beautiful they needed their own colour palette.

This was not something that anyone in the parlour seemed to understand. Foundation and base make-up was always applied as light a shade as possible no matter what colour the skin so that the person undergoing a make-over would almost always end up looking more like a geisha than anything else. This applied to bridal make-up in particular. Zainab had yet to see a bride who did not look like a pastry.

In fact, it seemed *de riguer* for Pakistani brides to look this way. It was a rare occasion when a bride came in and demanded subtle beauty rather than a full-on pancake experience. This was the standard of beauty, and anything less would be talked about and whispered about at the weddings. 'Did you see how little make-up she was wearing?' Or 'She was wearing *so* little jewellry,' or there wouldn't have been enough heavy embroidery on the bride's clothes and the like.

Zainab dreamt of make-overs she wanted to enact and brides that she wanted to make up to look totally different from any other women, she had ever seen in Pakistan. She noticed that the Pakistani fashion magazines seemed to be doing more and more interesting things, but she never actually saw this in her parlour.

Perhaps she needed to work at a different parlour. She had heard about a man who it was whispered was mad, flamboyant, some said gay, and she had seen him on the television. He had these wild, glittering eyes and was always surrounded by incredible men and women with the most beautiful hair and make-up she had ever seen. He was said to be the genius of his realm and was always doing crazy new things. Among the begums of her parlour he was talked about in dissaproving, hushed tones.

Often, whilst falling asleep in her small room, to the sounds of her brothers shouting at her mother, Zainab would dream that maybe she too could work for this mad genius one day, and finally get to try out her ideas.

'Zainab?' said Javed, 'Zainab?' She seemed to have wandered off in her mind somewhere, whilst relaying to him the behaviour of the women who came to the salon today. She looked at him as if suddenly realizing he was there and smiled, 'Yes Javed?'

'Are you okay?' *The poor dear man.* Zainab thought — he appeared genuinely worried about her.

'Yes, yes!'

'Javed?'

'*Ji* Zainab?'

'*Mein aap se aik request karna chatee hoon.* I have a request to make.'

'*Ji, ji keejiye*. Please go ahead'.

'Let's not go to the shrine tonight.'

'*Jo bhi aap chahe. Me aap ko ghar chor deta hoon?* As you wish. Should I drop you home then?'

'No.'

He looked at her quizzically. 'Then what?'

She looked embarassed, 'Can we drive around Defence or Clifton on your Vespa — just looking — at the beautiful houses, the cars —' she stopped in mid-sentence unsure if he would quite comprehend her request.

Javed felt his stomach lurch, could he have heard her correctly? Then before he knew what he was saying he blurted out, 'Only if we can count the number of air conditioner vents on the houses —'

She looked at him blankly for a second, and Javed panicked. Now she would think he was wierd.

But Zainab merely burst into laughter, shocked at her discovery that Javed knew exactly what she was talking about. She had never admitted to anyone to doing the same thing — asking puzzled rickshaw drivers to drive her around, hoping to catch a glimpse of one of the parties she had groomed her clientele for.

'What? What? I'm sorry...' stuttered Javed overcome with anxiety, 'It's just something I do sometimes.'

Zainab watched him talk and then for the very first time took his hand gently in her own and said, 'Javed I would love nothing more than to count air-conditioner vents with you. Let's go.'

* * * * * *

The End

Acknowledgments

The author would like to thank Aamer Hussein for his careful attention to these stories and help in sculpting them, Mohammad Hanif for believing in the stories and the city of Karachi, for always being unapologetically herself. Special thanks to my publishers Azad Ashim and Kashif Sharma-Patel for taking the stories forward.

In addition, I would like to thank:

Rukhsar Mukhtar, Amir Bux, Ali Hasan, Shalalae Jamil, Raania Durrani Azam Khan Durrani, Mariam Azmi, Mumtaz Mustafa, Adnan Malik, Anna Moorby, Nik Perring for providing vital resources at vital times.

Roohi Shoaib & Shelley Shoaib for constant enthusiasm and support for my writing.

Sakura Metcalfe, for all the joy.